BREAK FOR THE BORDER

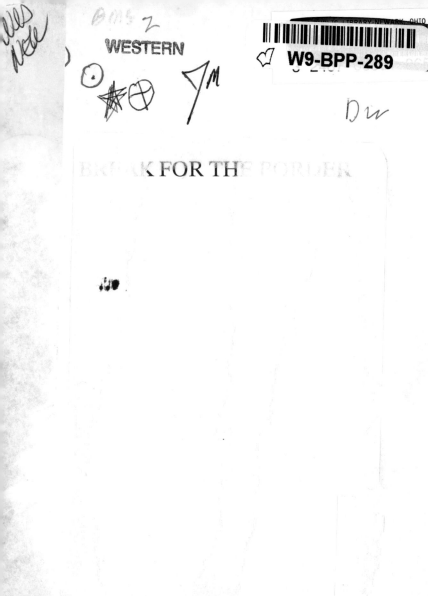

BREAK FOR THE BORDER

Frank Bonham

Chivers Press • G.K. Hall & Co.
Bath, England   Thorndike, Maine USA

This Large Print edition is published by Chivers Press, England, and by G.K. Hall & Co., USA.

Published in 1999 in the U.K. by arrangement with the author, care of Golden West Literary Agency.

Published in 1999 in the U.S. by arrangement with Golden West Literary Agency.

U.K. Hardcover   ISBN 0-7540-3747-9   (Chivers Large Print)
U.K. Softcover   ISBN 0-7540-3748-7   (Camden Large Print)
U.S. Softcover   ISBN 0-7838-8578-4   (Nightingale Series Edition)

The text of this Large Print edition is unabridged.
Other aspects of the book may vary from the original edition.

Set in 16 pt. New Times Roman.

Printed in Great Britain on acid-free paper.

British Library Cataloguing in Publication Data available

Library of Congress Cataloging-in-Publication Data

Bonham, Frank.
    Break for the border / Frank Bonham.
        p   cm.
    ISBN 0-7838-8578-4 (lg. print : sc : alk. paper)
    1. Large type books.   I. Title.
    [PS3503.O4315B74   1999]
    813'.54—dc21   99–19639

BREAK FOR THE BORDER

CHAPTER ONE

'What did he do, Daddy?' Jackson heard the labor contractor's daughter whisper. Jackson stood beside the wagon with the guard. They had just driven over from the prison labor camp. Clane, the guard, looked at the contractor and grinned.

'Oh, he was a dangerous man, Miss Clark,' Rip Clane said. 'But he's gentle now.'

The contractor and his daughter stood on the gallery of the long adobe house, above the prisoner and guard. 'No, Mr. Jackson wasn't a bad actor, Missy,' Warden Clark said. 'He wouldn't be here at our home if he was. Clane, take the shackles off him.'

Jackson raised his manacled hands toward the guard, who clubbed them down. 'If I want you to move, I'll tell you!'

On the other hand, Jackson knew, if he had not raised his hands Clane would have kicked him in the shin. Jackson's striped shirt, pants, and cap made him stand out like a bumblebee. Unshackled, he waited.

'Come here, Jackson,' the labor contractor said. 'I want you to meet my daughter.'

Clane cleared his throat and laid a hand on Jackson's arm as he started to move forward. 'Excuse me, Warden—' he said, with a frown. The guards all called Clark 'Warden,' which

1

was his function—to keep the convicts from wandering off from the mercury mine to which they were leased.

'You're excused, Clane,' Clark said. 'Drive the wagon over to the trees and shade the horse. Come forward, Jackson. That's fine—stand right there. Now, Jackson, this is my daughter, Missy. And Missy, this is the man Mr. St. Clair mentioned.'

'I'm pleased to meet you, Mr. Jackson,' the girl said. Her long skirts stirred as she moved forward a few inches. She wore her hair in ringlets, like little sausages, and looked as pretty, dainty, and useless as a hand-painted china teacup. The prisoner nodded at her, then spoke to Warden Clark.

'Clane didn't say what you wanted me for, Warden,' he muttered. As he spoke, he caught movement behind a window of the big adobe house, and a startling figure was visible for a moment: a woman all in black. Then she let the glass-curtain fall and was gone from sight.

'Do you like working in the mines?' The contractor winked, as if he had just cracked a joke. He had a handsome, fleshy face with a mustache shaped like an oxbow, a thick neck, and gray hair worn full and senatorial.

'Así así,' said Whit Jackson.

'Your trade was breaking horses, wasn't it?'

'Raising and training.'

'Would you like to train a horse for Missy?'

Dumbfounded, Jackson looked at the girl.

2

He was a man of medium height and slight build, underfed looking and beginning to lack in muscle bulk. He was several days overdue for a shave, and his sunken eyes stared like those of a corpse in a Civil War picture.

'What kind of horse?' he asked.

'A riding horse!' said the girl quickly. 'For my birthday. Daddy's going to let me ride.'

Why shouldn't he? Jackson wondered. But the warden was stingy with his favors. 'Tomorrow being Christmas,' the bull-guard had announced a few months ago, 'you'll only work a half-day.'

'Would this be after the day's work,' asked Jackson, 'or instead of it?'

'Instead.'

'Already got the horse, sir?'

'No, but there're several I'm looking at.'

Jackson felt the stubble on his chin. He wondered what the game was. His life was so full of bedbugs, infected cuts, hunger, and coughing up red dust that anything beyond these normal concerns puzzled him.

'I'd be glad to help,' he said, 'but I don't know why you don't buy a horse already trained.'

'Don't you, really?'

'I suppose you've had bad luck with a horse at some time, and you want a gentle-broke horse without bad habits.'

'That's it!' Missy said. 'And there isn't much choice of well-trained horses in Terlingua.'

3

Jackson squatted down to think. He made marks in the earth with a link of the chain hanging from his manacles. 'We're talking about quite a spell of time,' he said. (If he worked this right, he figured, maybe he could even get some meals at the warden's back door!).

'Well, you've got plenty, haven't you?' Clark smiled and nudged his daughter.

'You see, I don't rightly *bust* broncs, because I don't believe in savaging a good horse and tearing my lungs loose from my ribs. I've got my own methods. They take longer.'

'That's what your lawyer told me.'

Jackson glanced up. 'Was St. Clair here?'

'Last week. But you were underground when he came, and he couldn't wait. However, we had a good talk, and St. Clair was bragging on you. He told me a Jackson-broke horse is practically kept under glass, in your country. Where was it, now?'

'Knox County, south of Los Lobos.'

The girl asked curiously, 'What did you do, Mr. Jackson? Wrong, I mean.'

Jackson smiled, and the warden chuckled. 'Innocents abroad,' he said.

'I took some horses to Fort Collins,' Whit Jackson said. 'When I got there, there was some extras. We never got it cleared up how they got in my herd. So I came here to try to understand it.'

'Is that true—about the horses?' the girl

4

asked her father.

'I think so.'

'Why, I think that—!'

'Missy,' her father said, 'the man is going to train a horse for you. It is not going to be a series of social occasions, nor a legal action. Understand that.'

He raised his arm, and Rip Clane moved quickly to the wagon. He had been waiting a hundred feet away, among some very small dusty trees.

'All right, Jackson. I'll have some horses brought out in a few days, and get you to look them over. Then we'll see how it works.'

'There's just one thing,' Jackson said.

'Well?'

'Unless the girl plans to ride in prison clothes, I'd better work in an ordinary shirt and pants. A young horse will shy at anything freakish, and I think you'll admit these polecat suits are a little out of the ordinary.'

Clark regarded him stonily. 'Yes, and a man wearing one stands out in case he wanders off.'

'I know. But I know horses, too, and after a horse gets used to something like stripes, he may shy if somebody in ordinary clothes comes at him too fast.'

'Maybe you'd better wear a dress while you train the horse,' said the warden.

'Thought I'd better mention it,' said Jackson.

'Put your hands out, fool,' Clane said.

5

CHAPTER TWO

Is that a fact. Well what do you know. I hear O'Brien's leg got gangrenous and they cut it off. Gonzales, if you ever get near my cot again I'll kill you. Listen to this, men, Jackson's going to train a horse for Clark.

Statements as strong as these, and a lot stronger, were delivered in a dead mutter in the lease camp. It was done in order not to attract attention, and to keep one's personal feelings private. On the hike to the mine in the morning, Jackson talked to Bedbug Dunnigan, an old convict.

'Did you hear I got a chance to train a horse for the warden?'

'Watch out, Jackson, Clane's setting you up.'

'No, I think it was Clark's own idea. Clane was bucking.'

'Clane told your lawyer you refused to see him. Heard him as plain as you hear me.'

'Oh, that son of a bitch,' said Jackson. 'But I'll train the horse if I get the chance.'

'Watch out, Whit, don't even look like you knew there was a world out there. Don't say I didn't tell you. Why would Clark let you? Ask yourself that.'

'To get a safe horse for his daughter. She's the apple of his eye.'

'There it is, Whit, there it is. Didn't you

know her sister was killed in a fall? She was drug. Feller told me her mother's still in mourning five years after. If she ever gets a scratch Clark'll eat you for breakfast.'

'So that son of a bitch told Marcus I didn't want to see him. Comin' at you, Clane. Some day. Some—day.'

CHAPTER THREE

'The buckskin mare,' said Jackson. 'If price is no object.'

Four horses stood in the corral behind the barn. Jackson, wearing work pants and an old blue shirt the warden had come up with, the property of a dead prisoner, stood in the corral with the candidates for Missy Clark's riding horse. The girl stood on the bottom rail and rested her chin on the top one; Clark lounged beside her with his arms crossed, and Rip Clane, the guard, sat on the fence with his rifle across his knees. He was chewing on a cigar.

'How'd you know she was the dear one?' asked Clark.

'The seller is crazy if he's not asking at least seventy.'

'Eighty-five,' said the warden. 'But if that's the one, that's the one.'

For some reason Whit glanced at the house.

The gallery ran all the way around it, and he was quite sure he saw the warden's wife standing at a window watching what was going on in the corral. Old-timers in the prison said she was a plain lunatic, that she drank whiskey out of the bottle and screamed all night. Jackson believed she was half-mad all right, but in a quieter way. He was sorry for her.

'That mare will make the girl a fine horse,' he said. 'She could still be riding her fifteen years from now. But I have to say this. With any horse in the world, there's something that will spook it.

'I had an old blue roan that I could sit on its hocks, lay on it or under it, flick a rope between its legs, and fire off a gun by its head. But one day it broke a boy's leg. He walked behind it when it was rein-tied to a post, and it went hell-stokin' backward fifty feet before it slowed down. I don't know why. It never did it again. But I guess you know you can't guarantee a horse a hundred percent.'

'I'm not afraid!' Missy cried. 'Daddy— please!'

Jackson observed Clark start to look at the house, then clean his throat and say:

'Of course. I know that. Just do the best you can.'

'And if it ain't good enough, we'll find a way to tell you about it,' Clane said.

His red face was peeling, as usual, and looked redder than ever as he saw Jackson

8

getting away with it. He had a round head like a cannonball, a boozer's suety eyes, and a short and powerful body. He was afraid of the prisoners, Jackson believed, and thought that the only way to maintain control was to beat them, starve them, and bait them as much as possible. He saw Jackson as a troublemaker because the horse-trainer looked him in the eye. What he saw in Jackson might have been his ambition to get out of prison as soon as possible and—some day—to spend a half-hour alone with Rip Clane in an empty room.

Jackson did something now to infuriate the guard.

'If Clane could get the wagon now—' he said.

Clark drew a breath and looked stern. It was tantamount to an order—a prisoner giving an order to a guard! But the warden caught the message of Whit's almost imperceptible smile.

'Rip?' he said, and waggled a thumb at Clane.

The guard stared at Whit for a moment, then swallowed and climbed down. He said something to himself and kicked at a chicken feather on the ground as he crossed to the trees where he had left the horse and wagon.

'And maybe Missy would like to tell her mother the good news,' Jackson said, smiling at the girl.

'Yes!' she said eagerly, and raised her skirts to run toward the house.

The warden told Jackson: 'It's not the usual thing around here for a prisoner to send a guard on an errand, you know.' He stroked his handsome mustache and tried to make his face hard. But he was too inquisitive for it to work.

'I didn't mean it that way. Now, Warden, I don't expect favors in a place like this. We're here for correction. I understand that. I want to say, though, that I appreciate your picking me for the job.'

'I was in a corner, Jackson, and you looked like a mousehole. So it works both ways.'

'Fine. One thing I wanted to mention is that I believe Missy should learn to ride straddle. It's safer; she'll have control she wouldn't have sitting sideways, like on a couch.'

'I'll mention it. I could get her a pair of boy's Levi's—'

Jackson raised a finger in approval. 'And the first time she washes them, have her wear them till they dry, and they'll mold to her and she'll fit that saddle like skin. The other thing I wanted to say is this: I can't spend all day working with one horse, because I'd wear it out. So why don't you buy all four of these horses and let me train them?'

Clark laughed. 'Man, you *are* crazy! I can't afford to buy myself a whole remuda. Don't need another horse.'

'No, no—for resale,' Jackson said. 'Buy 'em rough, sell 'em trained. That strawberry roan would make a dandy saddle horse for a big heavy man. It would be like a carpenter building a house to resell, you might say. What he's selling is his labor. But in this case the labor wouldn't cost you a nickel.'

Clark's big Daniel Webster head turned as the wagon came rattling through Mrs. Clark's chickens toward the corral. He waved Clane off. 'In a minute, Rip,' he called. Clane glared in disbelief, then hung his head and looked at his lap. The warden bent down and ducked through the bars, joining Jackson inside the corral. He approached the buckskin mare and laid his hand on her. She held steady.

He said thoughtfully, 'I don't know what the Terlingua Mill and Mining Company would think about it. You're leased to the company by the State of Texas. I'd be making money on your labor, while the company was paying for your food.'

Whit Jackson worked a burr out of the mare's forelock.

'I've got it,' he said. 'Sublet me! The men say a prisoner brings eight dollars a month on lease. Why couldn't you pay the company that? Then the profit on the horses would be yours. And if you wanted you could set aside five dollars a head for me. Keep me from getting lazy.' He smiled. It made his unshaven cheeks look wide and gaunt.

Clark wagged his head. 'Jackson, you're as crazy as a bedbug,' he said.

Jackson looked at an ulcer on his wrist.

'Comes from living among them. Well, just thought I'd mention it, Warden.'

'I'll think about it. When do you want to start on the buckskin?'

'I already have. I whispered in her ear that she's beautiful,' said Jackson, with a wink. 'It never fails.'

'You damn fool!' laughed the warden. He beckoned Clane.

'Oh, and say,' Jackson added. 'If you *should* see a horse somebody's trying to get rid of—strong but dumb, like me—I might like to buy it, with what I make training horses.'

'What do you want with a horse, man?'

'Just the feeling of owning one, Warden. If I'm anything, it's a horse-trainer and raiser. It's just the feeling. Of plying your trade.'

* * *

As the wagon clattered across the long-shadowed, purplish flats toward the lease camp, Rip Clane scowled as though he had a terrible griping in his belly. His fingers bunched hard on the reins.

'I'm going to inform you on the geography of the Big Bend, Jackson,' he said. Jackson was riding backward on the wagon bed, shackled to a ringbolt. 'I don't think you quite get the picture. We're in the corner pocket of Texas down here. No town but Terlingua in a day's ride. Whores, whiskey, and beans, but no place

12

to hide. There's two rails that runs east to the mill. But the train don't go nowhere but that.

'South and west are the mountains and the river. And Mexico, of course. No prisoner's ever made it while I've been here. So don't figure on walking to Mexico or taking the railroad train when you leave.'

'No, no, Clane—I was planning on riding a horse. After I've served my time.'

'What did you tell the warden about me?' Clane demanded.

'Your name didn't come up.'

'What did you talk about, boy?'

'Clark asked me not to say.'

Clane's neck reddened, and the horse gave its head a toss. 'Keep it up, Jackson. It's going to be between you and I, eventually.'

'Probably. Some day.'

Jackson smiled at the pinkish evening light between them and a long butte, beyond which were higher buttes and then the blue silhouette of the mountains. They reminded him of the border hills near the horse ranch he had lost along with everything else. But for the first time in eighteen months he felt strength tingling in his fingers and forearms, like the beginning warmth of whiskey.

He held some cards, at last. But how to play them?

Clane halted the wagon and stood up, showing Jackson a small flat file. 'A prisoner hid this under a batten on the wagon bed

13

once,' he said. 'He managed to file off his shackles and made a run for it. He'll be in the mines till he dies.'

'I've got no reason to make a break, Clane,' Jackson said simply. 'Everything is copacetic. Why should I try to escape? In fact, Clark and Missy would have you flayed and soaked in brine if anything happened to me.' He smiled.

'You son of a bitch,' Clane said. He picked up the horsewhip and raised it. Jackson looked blankly at him. Clane finally said, 'Keep it up, boy!' He drove on.

CHAPTER FOUR

I hear Rip Clane got in a big fight in Terlingua last night.

No fooling. Who told you that?

Snake Eyes and Cox. They went with Clane and another guard to get provisions. After they loaded up the wagons Clane got drunk in a saloon and had the piss beat out of him.

He must be all show and no go—except with us prisoners. Looks tough enough, though.

He damn near kilt three men before somebody tapped him and all four of them ganged up on him.

What was the fight about?

The warden's daughter. He spoke of her as a little bitch. Can you beat that.

14

Why I thought he was inclined toward her. He looks at her like a dog looks at a pork chop.

That's just it, Jackson, he's inclined but you get the favors. A con like you. But I warn you, Whit, no good will come of it and a hell of a lot of bad.

I'm working again. That's good. I've got lady company. That's good. And I'm ridin' out of here on a horse.

You damn fool, when's that gonna be?

Some day, Bedbug.

Never, Whit. Not ever. You done made yourself too precious to Father Clark ever to get out while he's warden. Hadn't thought of that, had you, you dumb bastard.

CHAPTER FIVE

Missy in Levi's was something to behold.

She had done exactly what Jackson prescribed, with the result that the dark-blue denim had shrunk to her legs and bottom without a wrinkle. The copper rivets at the strain points were all that kept the material from splitting like the skin of a sausage. She had rolled the sleeves of her red-and-white checkered shirt to the elbows. She had done her hair up in a bun, and wore a small white scarf over it to protect her hair from the dust.

Jackson had changed from his skunk-stripes

15

in the barn, and when he emerged there she was waiting near the corral, looking as ripe and tender as a blue damson plum. Her eagerness illuminated her face. She smiled, waved at him, then bit her lip as if aware that she was revealing too much.

'I'm ready,' she said.

Jackson was ready, too, after eighteen months of batching. He would have to watch it, with Clane's eyes always on him and the guard out to settle. Where Jackson had lived the last year and a half, the most exciting thing was an occasional new stripe on a bedbug, and the thought of Missy Clark's breasts inside the boy's shirt was excruciating. He kept his eyes down as he walked toward her. Clane was lying on one elbow on the wagon bed, in the shade of the trees. His face was skinned and swollen, and he sweated and looked sick.

Jackson said, 'I'll need the oldest rope on the place—cotton is best—and an old saddle pad.'

Missy walked into the barn. Jackson heard Clane shout: 'Stay in sight, foolish!' He mounted the bars and looked the horses over. Someone had brushed the buckskin. Her tan summer coat looked oiled, her black mane and tail were clean. Missy came from the barn carrying a coil of cotton rope and an old saddle pad.

'Always did like a buckskin, no good reason,' murmured Jackson. 'Think you could outrun this mare?'

Missy giggled. ''Course not.'

'Think you could outkick her?' She shook her head. Her lips were parted, and her eyes danced. '*She* knows that, too. One way to tell her not to try outdoing you is to forefoot her— dump her on her nose a few times. Then snub her around the neck and choke her to a post till her eyes bug out.'

Missy looked stricken. 'I don't think I can watch, Whit. I hate to see an animal hurt. I—'

'I haven't hurt a horse in years, not on purpose,' Jackson assured her. He spoke quietly as he entered the corral through the bars. 'Easy, lady. Just going to play around for a while. Then I'll get a hackamore on you, and get you used to being handled. Okay? But there won't be any big day when I tie myself in the saddle, and an hour later my nose and ears are bleeding and we've got us a tame horse. No, ma'am. It's not gonna be like that.'

While he talked, he ran his hands over the little mare and found that she was already broke to a halter. He led her to a gate, down a chute to the riding ring, and Missy trailed along. The buckskin showed no nervousness.

'I think you'll like riding straddle,' Jackson said.

'I had to get a pair of boy's pants!' Missy blurted, and giggled. 'Mother helped me make the shirt last night. Daddy said, "How do you like that, Mother, your daughter has the figure of a twelve-year-old boy!"'

Jackson smiled. Well, not quite. He was not even quite sure the conversation had taken place. She was just making sure he noticed that twelve-year-old boys did not have figures like hers.

Oh, my God. This damn prison life, he thought.

*   *   *

Later he let Missy lead the horse around the ring while he worked with the other horses. Finally he led the mare to the barn. 'Clane would like it better if *you* tended her. He likes to be able to see me. Although I think he's asleep. He had a heavy night in Terlingua. Give her a quart of grain and some hay. And wipe her down good.'

At four o'clock the warden appeared on the road from the prison. Clane was getting the draft horse ready. Jackson called to him, 'I'm going to change my clothes now, guard.' Clane shrugged. Jackson pulled off his borrowed gloves and handed them to Missy.

'Will you put these with the rope and saddle pad?'

'Yes. Wait—!' The girl lowered her voice. 'I'll tell you a secret, Whit. Don't tell anybody, though. Your lawyer's coming!'

'When?' Unconsciously he slipped into a flat whisper.

18

'In three weeks.'

'Your father say it was okay?'

'Yes.'

'Anything else? Quick.'

'You sound so funny, Whit!'

He blinked. Smiled. 'It comes as a shock. I haven't seen anybody from home since—sure your father said it's okay?'

'Yes. It was Rip's idea not to let him see you last time. He said you'd been sassy to him. Daddy said he'll probably let Mr. St. Clair visit you right here.'

CHAPTER SIX

'Well, now, my boy. How are they treating you?'

'Can't complain, Marcus.'

'The food can't be too bad at the camp. You look fit enough.'

Jackson pushed his sleeves back and rubbed some bug ulcers. 'Clane and I take our dinners here lately. The warden's wife and daughter are good cooks. At the prison, Clane and I eat at the same mess, too. Would you say the food was tasty, Clane?'

Clane sat a few yards down the gallery, pulling flakes of sunburned skin off his nose, looking at them, and discarding them.

'Tasty enough for men doing time,' he said.

19

'Are you still filing appeals for me?' Jackson asked.

'There isn't much point, Whit,' said the old lawyer. 'Warden Clark tells me your record is clean, and that there's a good chance you'll be approved for parole in November. It would take longer than that to get another appeal started.'

'But if I don't make parole, I could still hope the appeal might go my way. That's what we live on here—hope.'

'I'll file if you wish. But if you shouldn't be approved for parole, then we can consider other—er—contingencies.'

Clane looked up in suspicion. 'What's that there "contingencies"?'

St. Clair raised his hands as though he were suspending a ruler between them. 'Possibilities,' he said.

He smiled. He was a huge old man in baggy pants and a rumpled white shirt creased with purple galluses. His black coat lay across the porch railing. Small, round, thick spectacles rested on the bridge of his pulpy nose. His eyes drilled into Jackson's. Listen to me! they said.

'All right, Marcus,' sighed Whit. 'Anything changed in Los Lobos?'

'Well, let's see. Sam Hatcher put John Simms on your old place. He's drinking a lot and pretending to be a horse-rancher.'

Whit frowned. 'Simms. Wasn't he in charge of the Army survey gang that ran some lines in the basin?'

'That's him. He still does a little surveying. And Lucha had word from Billy, finally.'

Billy Murphy was the husband of St. Clair's daughter, Lucha. He was a likeable fellow when he was sober, but could not settle down to anything. He had been chili-farming by the river when Whit first knew him and Lucha. Then, just before Whit went to prison, he had gone off to Mexico as a soldier of fortune. If the revolutionary general won, Billy Murphy would be rich!

'Billy was wounded in Puebla,' St. Clair said.

'My Lord! What's Lucha going to do?' A thrill ran through Jackson. He had been neighbors to the Murphys, and had had the misfortune to fall in love with Lucha Murphy the first time he saw her.

'Oh, he made it back. Now he's running for sheriff!'

'Well, it would be steady work.'

'And Lucha is still doing my paper work, thank heaven. She's been reading law with me since she was a little thing. Would you believe she's taken the bar examination now? At any rate, we've been working hard on a title matter; in fact, I'm on my way to Austin to do the final search.'

The mosquito-bar door opened, and Missy Clark brought out two plates of mulligan stew. Her dark, satiny hair hung below her shoulders. Jackson saw Clane's eyes feast on

21

her, like blowflies, then the guard stretched and smiled at the girl.

'Mama thought you all might like some stew,' she said.

'That'd be right nice,' said Clane. 'Nothing for my prisoner?'

Missy squeezed off a little smile as she went back for more.

The lawyer tasted his food and said: 'Very tasty. Pleny of chili. Made a little hunting trip in Mexico with Stu Perry last month, and we had some chili that would make angels weep, in a place called Casa Piedra.'

Jackson looked up quickly, then down.

'I'll take you over the same ground when you come back. Cap Rock to San Felipe, San Felipe to Palmitos, then back to the river at El Río. Thousands of quail.'

Jackson's head rang emptily, as though his ears were stopped up. Three of the places he had mentioned were north of the river, not in Mexico! Nor did Marcus hunt! So what had he been talking about? What was he trying to say?

Before he left, St. Clair said: 'Did you ever get the book on business practice that Lucha sent you?'

Clane grinned. 'He ain't on the list for parcels.'

'Well, that's too bad,' said the lawyer. 'She's bound to civilize you, Whit. Make a lawyer or big rancher out of you.'

'All the books in hell wouldn't make me any

more than I am—a horsebreaker,' Whit said. But he was angry to learn that he was not allowed to have parcels. He had written to St. Clair of certain things he would like to have. Probably his outgoing mail did not pass the censor either.

'Thanks for coming, Marcus. Be sure to get my appeal started, will you?'

'Consider it done. Lucha said the same thing—it may seem useless, but it will be one more thing to hope for.'

'Lucha's right.'

CHAPTER SEVEN

Every time Jackson worked with Missy and her horse, he saw Mrs. Clark at a window. He was reminded of the widows of fishermen in New England watching for ghost sails. At first she always stood, sometimes for an hour; then he could tell that she was sitting in a chair, just observing the girl lie across the mare, lead it with the bridle it now wore, and run it around the ring at the end of a long rope. The girl fed it, brushed it down, dug pebbles out of its hoofs, did everything but sleep with it. She saddled it, finally, with a loose cinch, and within a week it was time for the horse to be ridden.

Jackson rode it around the ring. It was as

good a horse as he had ever worked with. It was already rein-wise, responding to a rein laid across its neck rather than to a pull on the bit.

'Whit, *when* do I get to ride her?' Missy pleaded, almost in tears one morning.

'Sometime,' Jackson said.

'You always say "sometime"! What if I told you your lawyer was coming to see you again— *sometime?*'

'When?' he asked quickly.

'When do I get to ride her?'

Jackson tightened the cinch a little and patted the mare's neck. Then he slipped his arms around her neck and swung beneath her. The horse glanced down at him as though he were a strange sort, but did not flinch. He went back and pulled on her tail.

'I'd like to speak to your mother, Missy,' he said.

Missy turned her head away from him. 'She'll say no.'

'Have you ever asked her?'

'I've tried to. But she always starts crying. I haven't for a long time. Daddy and I decided this together. We thought it might help her. I don't know.'

'She's wearing a white shirtwaist this morning. That's a change. Maybe she's ready.'

'She is?' Missy peered at the window. 'She's changed since we started, then.'

'Maybe her mind, too. I'll just go up and pay my respects through the window.'

After leaving the ring, Jackson called to Clane, 'I'm going to speak to Mrs. Clark through the window.'

'Why, foolish?'

'Missy's idea. To ask permission for her to ride.'

Clane tossed one hand in bafflement. Jackson went on.

He walked to the house, climbed the back steps, and took off the flat gray hat some other dead prisoner had bequeathed him. He stood near the window and the woman sitting near it. Her eyes looked large, her face thin. Because of the lace curtain, she appeared misty, as though wearing a veil.

'Mrs. Clark,' Jackson said, 'I just wanted to pay my respects.'

'Thank you, Mr. Jackson,' the woman said, in a surprisingly clear voice.

'I'd like your permission to let Missy ride this morning.'

'You'd do it anyway, Mr. Jackson. Isn't that true?'

'Yes, if she still intends to. She's doing it for you.'

'Me!'

'Because you're on the wrong road, Mrs. Clark. It doesn't lead anywhere. You're in prison, like me. Once you get over the shock, you'll feel better. She and your husband believe that, and so do I.'

'Tell her it's all right,' said the woman. 'I

know young girls have to take chances, like anybody else. You seem like a sensible man, Mr. Jackson. I'm surprised you let yourself get in prison.'

'I got in with a bad crowd, ma'am,' Jackson said.

It wouldn't hurt for her to think he was being reborn by the horse-training experience. Maybe he was.

*   *   *

He showed Missy the proper way to mount—the stirrup turned backward for her toe—and gave her a boost. Sitting in the saddle, she looked eager and proud. She fluttered her fingers at the house. Jackson led the horse around the ring a few times, and then let the girl have the horse. In the prison wagon, he saw Clane sitting up straight.

Missy rode for an hour. When she got off, she was stiff but still flushed with excitement.

'She's adorable!'

'You've got yourself the best riding horse in West Texas.'

'Since I was twelve I've dreamed of riding! I've always felt like an old lady in that buggy. Oh, Whit!' She sniffled and leaned her head against him. Shocked, he moved away and took the catch rope from the fence.

'Don't do that. Take her in the barn now and tend her. She's your horse now. I've got these others to work with.'

'Mr. St. Clair is coming Thursday!' Missy whispered.

*   *   *

'Tomorrow,' Jackson told Clane, as they rattled back to the prison, 'I'll work in my polecat suit.'

'Why? Thought the whole idea was to get the horse used to regular clothes?'

'Tomorrow I'm taking the girl riding. It's your promise that I'm coming back.'

'Oh, no you don't, fool! That's one the warden *won't* buy.'

'She can't go riding alone. So who's going to go with her? You? Okay, that leaves me alone at the house. Would the warden allow that? Or leave me in the mine while you take her riding. Who's going to train his horses? Think about it, Clane.'

Clane cursed him up and down, back and forth, but said no more about it.

CHAPTER EIGHT

Missy was almost too lame to ride the next day, but she was game for it. Riding the strawberry gelding he had rough-broken to the saddle, Jackson took her out in a big circle

27

around the buildings. He wore his prison clothes. She was like a child, exclaiming on the power in the horse's movements. Her hair was combed back in a braid and tied with red yarn. After an hour, they returned and Jackson got to work with the other horses.

That night he and Clane met the warden as he was riding home from the prison. They stopped to talk.

'To hear my daughter tell it, you'd think she had the best riding horse in Texas, Jackson,' Clark said.

'She may just have. The strawberry will be ready in another couple of weeks. I'm riding him already. Who raised the buckskin?'

'A man named Sample, other side of town.'

'If he's got any other good ponies, better buy a couple. I won't be spending much time with the buckskin any more.'

'Still want a plug of your own to work with?'

Jackson saw the guard turn his head to stare at him. Then Clane took a deep breath and looked across the lavender hills.

'I'd like that, Warden. Just something rough, but healthy.'

A half-mile from the prison, Clane cursed. 'Goddamn horse is going lame!' He unshackled Whit. 'Right foreleg,' he said. 'Lift it and let me see the hoof.'

Jackson saw no swelling, nor was the horse holding a hoof at the wrong angle. He bent over, and with his shackled hands lifted the horse's foreleg between his knees. Clane's boot crashed into his rump like a cannonball. He fell against the horse, which kicked him and shied, snorting. Jackson fell and rolled away, with a pain like a knife in his ribs. When he breathed, the pain made him groan. He came to his knees, his face waxy, both hands pressed against his broken rib.

Clane was laughing. 'You damn fool! Did you think I was serious? Just hoorawing!' The guard had kicked him in the rump with all his force, and the horse had done the rest. 'Get back in the wagon.'

* * *

Bedbug and another man lashed a torn blanket tightly around his chest that night. He could scarcely breathe, but the pain was less with the rib immobilized.

'Coughed up any blood?'

'No.'

'Thank God, then. Are you gonna tell Father Clark? He'd likely whip Clane's ass for him.'

'How would Mrs. Clark take it if she found out Missy's horse-trainer had been hurt by a horse. If that woman gets upset she could wreck the whole thing.'

'That might be the best thing for you Romeo. Are you fallin' for that girl?'

'Not exactly. I've already got a girl. Married

29

to somebody else . . .'

Bedbug laughed heartily, without making a sound.

CHAPTER NINE

'I don't know much about you, Whit.'

A half-mile from the house, Jackson held the reins of the mare, leading the little horse while the girl walked. She was resting, still sore. He was plenty sore, too, but couldn't let it show, for fear of its damaging his plan.

'What do *I* know about *you*?' he replied.

'There's nothing to know about girls like me. My father was the jailer in Houston until five years ago. Then he got a chance to come here. They'd been losing so many prisoners the State was going to stop leasing to Terlingua. We came here, and I hated the loneliness. I still do. Then my sister went for a ride with a boy and—and everything's been like a perpetual funeral since.'

'That's all there is to tell?' asked Jackson. 'What about a young girl's hopes and dreams?'

'I dream of being the most beautiful woman in Texas, and raising the most beautiful horses. Bankers and congressmen will ride my horses.'

'You're halfway there on that dream,' Jackson said. (Wouldn't hurt to keep her on his team.)

She looked up at him, then down. 'I'm halfway sorry I got you to train the horse for me,' she said. 'Are you married, Whit?'

He faltered, rubbing his sore rib. 'No.'

Missy peered into his eyes. 'But you're in love with your lawyer's daughter!' she blurted.

He laughed. 'Now, where did you hear that?'

'Admit it! She's sent several parcels that Daddy couldn't let go through. And I heard Mr. St. Clair talking about her and her husband.'

'She feels sorry for me. Wouldn't you?'

'But she's married!' Missy protested.

'Sure. And her husband is probably sheriff of the town I used to live in, by now. Does that mean I'm in love with her?'

Missy pouted but finally smiled.

'You've never told me how you got in trouble, Whit,' she said. 'What happened?'

'The trial record says I started for Fort Collins with thirty horses and got there with forty-one. The other eleven belonged to Los Lobos Land and Cattle Company, and I couldn't prove I hadn't stolen them.'

'But if they were in your herd?—'

'One night two men threw in with my Mexican helper and me, just two days before we reached the fort. They asked leave to string along. In the morning they were gone, so we took the horses along. Some Rangers took me in custody. They'd had a telegram about some

31

stolen horses.'

'Why, that's awful!'

'If you believe me, you're one of the first people who has. It's a ridiculous story.'

'Whit, why would they *do* it?'

'It was over some land I homesteaded. Shafter and Drum had run stock on it for years, although it's rightly Government land. Along with half the rest of the county. They had to make an example of me, in case anybody else got to looking over their metes and bounds. So I got sent here.'

'Poor Whit,' Missy said. And then, softly: 'If you got down off your horse, I don't think Clane could see you.'

Jackson swept the sky with a glance, watching some buzzards, and finished by studying the long slope leading up to the ranch. He could see the roofs of the barn and house but no indication of the guard. He swung down. Missy waited between the horses.

'You're how old?' Jackson asked.

Her eyes closed; she said, 'Seventeen last month.'

Jackson sighed. 'Well, as long as I'm already in prison—'

She gasped when he pulled her against him. He could feel every inch of her body. He kissed her, and ran one hand up to her throat; he felt a pulse throbbing. Then he dug his fingers into her back and felt the ribs under them. Then he suddenly stepped back, walked away, picked up a rock, and threw it.

Missy moved to the off side of her horse and turned the stirrup as he had taught her. They rode back, looking innocent. Jackson decided that for various reasons it must not happen again. It could lead nowhere. She could only get hurt, and he might get hurt as well.

CHAPTER TEN

Weeks passed before Marcus St. Clair came again, but at last he arrived one afternoon. They sat on the porch for their visit. St. Clair sponged his face with a wadded handkerchief. He looked more florid than Whit had ever seen him, and he seemed breathless.

'Lordy! Bless you for the cold tea, ladies,' he said, smiling at Missy and her mother. Mrs. Clark sat in a rocker and Missy on the top step.

'We enjoy such charming company, Mr. St. Clair,' Mrs. Clark said coquettishly.

A few yards away, Rip Clane got up from his chair. 'Excuse me, Mrs. Clark,' he said. 'Your husband said a half-hour, and it's been forty minutes. So if you'll—'

'Oh, do sit down, Rip,' sighed the warden's wife. 'And how did your business go in Austin?'

she asked St. Clair.

Whit listened eagerly for a clue to what the lawyer had really been talking about last time.

'Quite well, thank you. It's a case in which I represent a Mexican gentleman with holdings in our area. His name is Lopez y Durán...' He rambled on like a patient old horse, explaining a complicated boundary matter involving some Government land. But Whit listened carefully, because Lopez y Durán was the governor of a Mexican state across the border from Los Lobos, and he did not own land in Texas!

What land was St. Clair talking about?

The Los Lobos Basin, which was claimed by the United States? But it had been American land ever since a boundary commission arrived at that arrangement twenty years ago, following a flood during which a small stream had wandered south from the main river and encircled a large tract of land before wandering back to the Big River.

Clane rose again. 'Okay, that's it, folks. This man has work to do.'

'Sit down, Rip, do. My stars. Oh, look— there's a buggy coming from town,' Mrs. Clark said, fanning herself with a handkerchief. 'Now, who would that be?'

Jackson saw the buggy come rattling over a rise a quarter-mile from the ranch house. St. Clair sighed.

'I'm afraid,' he said, 'that it's my daughter.'

Jackson turned his head quickly.

'But why didn't you tell us she was with you?' asked the warden's wife.

'Frankly, I didn't want to jeopardize Mr. Jackson's situation with too many guests.'

St. Clair said to Whit: 'Lucha's been helping me with the title search on the Lopez y Durán matter. She went up to Austin with me . . .'

Jackson did not look at Missy. His rib throbbed as he took a breath too deep for the healing bone. He began to tingle with excitement, but was anxious, too. Marcus St. Clair had had better judgment than Lucha. But of course neither of them had known about Missy's interest in him. This might be disastrous.

The girl stopped the horse below the porch, dropped the stone-anchor, and looped the reins about the whipstock. She smiled at the group on the porch as she pulled off her driving gloves.

'I'm sorry to have gone against your wishes, Father,' she said. 'But it didn't make sense to be in Terlingua and not say hello to Whit— May I join you?' she asked Mrs. Clark.

The warden's wife rose politely. Lucha came up the steps and Marcus made the introductions. 'Mrs. Clark, Missy—my daughter, Maria de la Luz Murphy. We call her Lucha. Named after a Mexican great-aunt, you see. And Mr. Clane.'

Rip brought her his chair and Lucha sat

35

down. She was dark-haired, but with gray eyes and warm skin. She was rather tall, and slender. Her thin summer gown was gray, with white piping. She smiled at Whit, but there was anguish in her eyes. He knew he must not look as good as he had thought.

'How are you, Whit?' she asked.

'Sound as oak. I've got a special job. Maybe Marcus told you. I'm training horses.'

Pink and excited, Missy came in. 'You must see the little mare he trained for me! Do you have time to watch her work?'

'I'm afraid I don't. I must make the most of what little time I have. But if anybody could train a riding horse, it would be Whit. You're fortunate.'

Whit moved in quickly. 'Marcus tells me Billy had a bad time in Mexico.'

'He was foolish enough to hire on with a revolutionary army! But he's home, safe, and now he's been elected sheriff. And already talking about a treasure hunt in Sonora. So I'm running the farm, more or less alone.'

'Billy has the seven-year itch,' said St. Clair. 'And he's bound to scratch it all over Mexico.'

'Mrs. Clark,' said Lucha, 'I'm puzzled that Mr. Jackson can't have parcels or mail. Why is that?'

'It's the warden's policy,' Mrs. Clark said in her gentle way. 'This is not a prison, you see, it's a labor camp. And some of the camps have had so many escapes that they're trying a new system of no mail. With some of the men, at least.'

'But why this man?'

'Hey, hey! I've got the world by the tail,' Whit said. 'Nobody here but us chickens.' *Don't ruin my arrangements!* he was trying to tell her.

'Ought to get you some convick lease-labor like Jackson for your farm, Miz Murphy,' said Clane. 'Goes for eight dollars a head per month. Cheaper'n a mule!'

Lucha gazed past him, stonily.

'Whit,' she said at last, 'you must not let what's happened change the way you feel about yourself. You are the same man you were.'

'Oh, better!' Jackson said. 'Travel has broadened me.'

'Don't put your mind too much on travel, boy,' said Clane with a laugh.

'And of course your hearing comes up soon, and we'll pray that you're approved for parole.'

St. Clair slapped his thighs and said, 'Well, ladies! Thank you for your hospitality. Whitman, my boy—you're in good hands.'

He offered Whit his hand. Whit felt a tiny cylinder between their palms. St. Clair let him get a grip on it with two fingers before he pulled his hand away. 'I'll come up and listen in on the hearing,' he said.

Whit closed his hand on the little

matchstick-thick roll of paper. Lucha held his hand in both of hers, and spoke in a low voice, with tears in her eyes.

'Don't let them change you, Whit! Do your damndest!'

Then she went down the steps and drove away. Missy gazed after her, thoughtfully. Whit put on his horsebreaking hat and, with a sigh, followed Clane back to the corral.

*   *   *

That night he unrolled the tiny cylinder of paper.

It was a tiny India ink copy of a topographical map of the Big Bend region. Five landmarks had been ringed with red ink. He was not sure what the map meant yet, but hid it in his belt. What he thought it meant was that St. Clair was not very hopeful of the parole hearing's going his way and that he was developing an alternate plan for him.

CHAPTER ELEVEN

'Well, I can't say you didn't tell me,' Missy told him the next time they went riding.

'You're holding the reins too tight,' Whit said. 'Easy does it.'

'With a man, or a horse?'

Whit laughed and, reaching out, took her hand. 'Hey! She was married when I first met her. She's still married. I used to help out on their farm now and then, when her husband was away and something needed doing.'

'She loves you,' Missy said bleakly.

'She loves crazy Billy Murphy.'

'She came all this way to visit you.'

'You weren't listening to her father. She's been helping him on this land case, and she went to Austin with him on the title search. She's lawyer, too. So why not visit me on the way back?'

Missy sighed. 'Oh, I know. But I still think she loves you. Do you love her?'

Whit leaned over and kissed her cheek, then glanced back in the direction of the house. Fortunately, it, and Clane, were out of sight. 'Missy, if I weren't a convict, and hoping to be an *ex*-convict, I'd have proposed to you a long time ago. But just think about what we have here. Do you see yourself married to an ex-convict?'

'We could go away—'

'And raise horses someplace where nobody will loan me a nickel to get started?'

'My—my father will loan you some money—'

'To an ex-con? Oh, no. Let's just keep our heads, Missy, and hope for the best.'

CHAPTER TWELVE

Whit broke and trained horses all summer and through the fall. He never went down into the mines again. And he never got a letter—from Lucha, Marcus, or anyone.

Clane began bringing along a canteen of water laced with rum or brandy, so that by night he was flushed and sleepy. Clark offered him a bull-guard's job; the pay was a little better, but he stuck with his lazy job and Mrs. Clark's cooking.

A week before the parole hearing, Clark came home early one chilly afternoon and took Missy riding. They returned in a raw and windy dusk. The girl was chilled and excited, her face reddened with cold. She dropped the split reins and raised her hands to show how the mare stopped dead when the reins fell. Whit, brushing down a horse, shook his head in reproof.

'Don't ever do that again,' he told her. 'Suppose something spooked her right now?'

Across the way, he saw Clane clambering onto the wagon seat and heard him belch. Jackson reached up to help Missy down, felt her hand squeeze his own. The warden dismounted.

'Missy,' he said sternly.

Whit went tense, afraid he had seen the hand-squeeze.

'What, Daddy?'

'See if your mother needs help in the kitchen.'

Missy looked puzzled, but went off to the house, trim as a colt. Jackson waited, uneasily. He began unsaddling the buckskin. The warden spoke.

'Next Wednesday's your big day,' he said.

'Yes, sir!' No harm in sounding cheerful, Whit hoped. 'Will St. Clair be allowed to sit in on it?' He hoisted the saddle onto a corral bar. In the wind raking across the buttes and hills from the canyons of the Rio Grande, he could taste juniper thickets and chino grass.

'We'll see,' said the warden. 'What I wanted to ask you was this: Would you like to work for me?'

'How's that?'

'Breaking and training horses, man, just like you've been doing—only for fifteen dollars a head. That is top dollar, Jackson, and you know it. You'd board in town and come out every day.'

'Warden, I—this is a surprise. But I've got some land to go back to. I'd like to do that, I think. Try to pick up again.'

'Thought you ran into trouble over that land before?' Clark's fleshy, mustachioed face was stern and red. He carried his head forward on his shoulders and had somewhat the look of a bull sea lion.

'No, sir. It was horses. The land's still there.'

'I see. You really mean you don't like

41

working for me, isn't that it?'

'No, sir! Working for you has been the only good thing that's happened to me lately. But I s'pose any man would rather work for himself.'

'In other words, you admit it! You don't like working for me.'

Too late Jackson felt the ground caving away. 'No, that's not it at all! But I like my independence, you see. Still, I reckon it'd be smart to work for somebody else for a while and collect a stake, wouldn't it? Well, sure, I'll be glad to.'

Clark's eyelids slowly closed and slipped open, like those of a dozing hawk. 'On second thought, I'm not sure it would be the best thing for Missy. No, I'm sure it wouldn't. Forget it. I think she may have taken a liking to you, and I don't want to subject her to any attachment to an ex-convict.'

In agony, Jackson said: 'No, sir, I don't believe that's true! She admires the way I trained her horse, and she's high about coming along as a rider. But as far as it bein' me goes—'

'Good night, Jackson,' the warden said.

CHAPTER THIRTEEN

'Good luck, Whit. You damn fool. You'll need plenty now.'

Bedbug said that, hacking and spitting as the fall-out bell rang for the miners. Some of the prisoners—cooks, clerks, and camp mules—had already left the adobe barracks. The miners shuffled from dark holes in the adobe buildings—unbarred cubicles with rifle slots for windows. Little light entered, but during the summer the sun glaring on the corrugated iron roofs made ovens of the cells. In summer only the tunnels were cool. But in winter the cold blasts from the north chilled the cells.

Jackson groomed himself before the triangular scrap of mirror in the cell he and Bedbug shared with three other men. Clark had promised shaves to the men who were coming up for parole hearings, but the barber had not shown up. Razors were not permitted. But aside from a quarter-inch black stubble, he appeared well fed, and his eyes had lost the old corpse-like stare. He could have been any mustanger just in from a week's horse-trapping.

A guard named Krebs sat in a chair tipped back against the wall of the camp business office. A shotgun lay across his knees.

'You-all line up,' he said. 'Nobody's here yet.'

The wind blew grit over the ground. Whit managed to be last in line, figuring that after five mangy convicts had passed before them, the parole board might think he looked

43

relatively guiltless.

Clark and three other men arrived in a hack rented from a livery stable in Terlingua. On the seat with the warden was Marcus St. Clair.

'Father Clark looks right feisty about something,' said Krebs, as a prisoner took charge of the horse. 'Bad day for you men, I expect.'

St. Clair smiled at Whit. Clark never looked at him. Nor did the two men in black who sat on the back seat. One was extremely tall and walked humped over. The other was a hard-eyed man who wore a flat Momon hat. They all went inside.

The prisoners waited, a couple of them smoking their pipes.

The door opened. Clark beckoned the first man in line. He was gone only about three minutes. He came out, turned up the collar of his jacket, and walked off. That was the signal that he had been turned down—the collar.

'Johnson.' Clark read the name from a sheet of paper, then went back inside.

Johnson emerged in a few minutes, turned up his collar, and shuffled away.

At last Whit's name came up. Krebs beat softly on his thighs, grinning. 'Whoo-ee!' he said. 'Five down and one to go.'

Three desks had been lined up, and Clark and the prison officials sat at them. There were several chairs against the adobe brick wall. Jackson was given no instructions, so he

44

waited, erect, against the wall. St. Clair sat at the end of the row of chairs. Behind Clark on the other wall were crossed flags of the U.S. and the State of Texas. There were papers before the men. They read the brownish script and shot glances at Jackson.

'Robert Whitman Jackson,' Clark read out.

'Camp behavior?' asked the tall man, who had a bald and knobby head, like a vulture.

'No marks since the first month,' said Clark.

'Violence?'

'No. The question,' said Clark, 'is one of attitude, and sufficiency of time served. Eleven felonies, one per horse.'

'I see,' said the husky man, who had the face of a thug. 'And only two years served?'

Whit's fists clenched and unclenched. St. Clair said quickly: 'The sentence was only thirty months, gentlemen, and with good behavior—'

Clark glanced right and left at his colleagues, then at the lawyer. 'I said you could listen. I didn't say you could represent him. What do you think, gentlemen?'

'Are you aware,' the man with the bony head asked, 'that you are here because you committed eleven serious crimes?'

'I'm here,' Jackson said, 'because I couldn't prove I was innocent.'

'Hush,' St. Clair mumured.

'You are here because you were proved guilty! That is how the law functions! I don't like your attitude worth a damn, Whitman.'

'Jackson,' murmured Whit.

'Be quiet! Jackson. I think another year might be worth ten years of freedom to you. Years when you'd think twice before stealing another horse.'

Jackson turned up his jacket collar and walked out.

*   *   *

Rip Clane was waiting outside. 'All right, you damn fool,' he said. 'You horsed us both out of a good thing.'

'Not as far as I know. Only myself.'

Clane gave him a short, hard jab in the belly. Whit was unprepared for it and went down gasping. 'You know now!' Clane said. 'Clark's sold all the horses, including yours. You're back in the pit.'

CHAPTER FOURTEEN

But a week later Clane called him out again at the muster bell. Clane roosted on the seat of a camp wagon and had manacles in his hands. 'Climb up, horsethief!' he said happily.

'What's going on?'

'Things are back to normal.'

On the way to the warden's home Clane

explained that Clark had traded Jackson's horse for three raw broncs, and that he had bought two more.

'And you're lucky,' said Clane. 'Your lawyer come over and made a special plea to Father Clark. He stayed around town a few days waiting for the stage out of here. You want to know something else, fool? You'll be lucky if you *ever* get out of here. You made yourself too valuable to Clark. You're the only chicken in camp, and he's going to keep you busy laying.' Clane went into prolonged laughter.

Whit started in on the horses. They were not worth much. The warden must have bought them from a traveling horse-trader. The only horses in sight worth a nickel were Clark's gelding and Missy's buckskin. Clark should have let him pick them as before.

Missy did not appear until mid-afternoon. The shadows of the winter afternoon were running across the yard. She wore a sheepskin coat of her father's that came to her knees, and had tied a blue kerchief over her hair. Whit, working with a bony black horse that would give its riders a sore neck every time it went out, watched her bridle her horse and lead it to the fence where she had placed her saddle.

'Mama says she'd like you to go riding with me,' she said. 'I've been so restless lately she says I make her nervous.'

'What'll I ride?' Whit asked.

47

'Daddy's horse. He's using the buggy this week. So many papers to carry. They're getting ready for a State inspection.'

Jackson called to Clane. 'I'm taking Missy riding!'

Clane waved. The rum-and-canteen trick kept him happy. Jackson saddled the gelding and they rode out.

'What happened?' Missy asked, looking straight ahead as they rode toward a fluted, dun-colored butte.

'They decided I wasn't ready.'

'Or my father did?'

'He didn't disagree.'

'What will you do?'

'Train horses. It beats the mine.'

'He sold your horse.'

'So I heard.'

'And now he has a contract with an Army post. Thirty horses over the next year. He must plan on your being here, Whit.'

'Looks that way.' Jackson remembered the map. He wondered if he could follow the trail St. Clair had drawn on it. Maybe, but it was a full day's ride and more, at a lope, and he wouldn't have a day's worth of loping horses. He hoped St. Clair knew that a man with a single horse could not outdistance a posse with remounts.

Missy pulled up. She put one hand to her face and he saw that she was crying. He patted her arm. But there was nothing comforting to say, not when things were hopeless and her father was the reason.

'It's cruel!' she said, sniffling. 'I don't know when he'll ever let you go. He can keep you here forever.'

'Now we're both beginning to realize how it works,' Jackson said. 'A man's better off being useless and half-crazy, like Bedbug. If you've got anything they want, they'll keep you.'

'No, they won't.' Missy wiped her eyes and looked at him. 'It isn't far to Mexico. Only, if you were caught!—'

Jackson smiled. 'That's what we think of when we're done killing bugs at night. It's not far, *but*—You kill them with matches,' he said. 'Light them and run them along under the frame of your cot. They pop and fall off.'

Missy held his hand and closed her eyes. 'I'm going to break a law now,' she said. 'Mr. St. Clair whispered to me as he was leaving, "The morning of January third." That's all.'

'That's next month!'

'Yes. He must have decided that it was hopeless, too.'

'Then he must have decided that I wanted to live the rest of my life in Mexico. I don't see how I can go back. But there's a big town called San Felipe, across a river from ours. Should think they'd extradite me, though . . . Well, I got time to think about it.'

*　　　*　　　*

49

He was still thinking about it two weeks later, when Missy told him the bad news. Lucha had written him that her father had died shortly after returning home.

CHAPTER FIFTEEN

Clane reined up before the barn and set the brake on the wagon. The ratchet made a sound like bones breaking. This was the day St. Clair had named for the escape try. Jackson did not meet the guard's eyes as he unshackled him; he was afraid he would see his nervousness. Missy was struggling to haul a cart of stable litter from the barn. Excitement ran through Whit's veins like ants.

He had decided to go ahead with the plan, if he got a chance. *What have I got to lose?* he asked himself.

He would gamble that Lucha knew about her father's plan, that—somehow—she would be able to make it work. She had courage and determination, and if she knew how it was supposed to go . . .

Clane called to Missy, 'Hey there, little one! Let me do that for you.'

'Oh, I don't mind,' Missy said.

Whit swallowed. His throat was as dry as chalk. Did she remember it was today? Was she going to help?

'Now, you leave it be, hear?' Carrying the rifle, Clane sauntered across the yard.

'Thank you, Rip. That's very nice of you.' Missy rubbed her palms together.

Clane pulled the cart behind the barn to dump it near Mrs. Clark's kitchen garden. Jackson entered the corral and stood regarding the horses speculatively. In winter Missy's horse and her father's were always stabled in the barn, to prevent their growing heavy winter coats. As he examined a horse's hoof for pebbles, Whit saw Clane come back, put the rifle in the cart, and push the cart into the barn. Missy smiled at Clane as he passed, then she stood beside the door in the chill sunlight. Briefly, she touched Clane's arm.

'Thank you, Rip.'

A few moments later, the girl walked toward the house. 'Hurry!' she murmured to Whit as she passed the corral. She had not forgotten!

Jackson ducked through the bars and went toward the barn. In the shadows he made out Clane shoveling stable litter into the cart from a stall. The rifle was out of sight. Then he saw it leaning against a stanchion, at least ten feet from the guard! Clane peered around sharply.

'Did you see my work clothes?' Jackson mumbled.

But Clane moved immediately toward the gun. Jackson ran toward it. Clane yelled, 'You

51

damned—!' His hand closed on the barrel, just as Jackson swung.

'*Now*—*!*' Whit said. 'Now, you bastard!'

Clane stumbled away with a groan. The rifle fell to the floor. Jackson seized it and tossed it near the door. Then he went after the guard. Clane was staggering, his brains addled by the shot he had taken to the cheekbone. Whit hit him in the belly and the man dropped to his knees and doubled over gagging. He pulled him up again, writhing, and shoved him against the wall. Then he made several hard chops at his face, breaking his nose, cutting an eye, and opening a gash on his chin. Clane's head rolled loosely, and Whit let him fall.

He gagged him with his own handkerchief and a string from a sack and tied him in a stall. Then he yanked his work clothing from a hook and changed. Carrying Clane's rifle and a saddle, he walked to Father Clark's horse and saddled it. He led the horse from the barn. He shot an anxious look toward the house, and saw no one at the window. Then he rode from the yard, southwest toward his first landmark, without hearing a sound from the house. *God bless you, Missy!*

Whit, you damned fool. You'll never make the river. There's mountains and canyons. Even if you do, the posse will cross and bring you back.

Bedbug had told him that last night as Whit studied his little map. Maybe he was right.

Certainly Whit had little idea of what he was supposed to do, but he would ride to his first landmark and see what he found.

For a half-mile he jogged through dry creekbeds in the red-streaked cinnabar hills, then let the horse into an easy lope. It was supposed to be twelve miles to the camp called Round Corral. He could lope and jog the horse that far, but after that it would be a slow ride. Slow for anyone following him, too, unless they brought extra horses. Marcus, I hope you knew what you were doing. I hope Lucha knew, too. If they get an early start on me, they may ride me down. They know the trail and I don't. That little bitty map! *Round Corral. Joe Spring. Horse Camp. Panther Spring. Alamito Creek.*

I hope they've got signs on them so I'll know!

CHAPTER SIXTEEN

The trail was plain enough, though relatively untraveled. It wound like a snaketrack through arroyos covered with candelaria and agave, climbing through the first range of hills. His spirits rose. He had not been off that damn desert in two years! From the crossing he squinted back through the cold clear air toward the town. Terlingua was seven or eight

53

miles distant now, but he saw dust at two points on the trail.

The chase had started! They'd bring remounts, so they could travel faster than he.

He headed the horse down a narrow valley between the hills and a long mountain range. He traveled straight up and down in the saddle, blending with the movements of the horse, making it easy on it. The gelding was breathing deeply.

Below him he caught a glimpse of a camp. A horse in a stone corral—the ruins of an adobe—a drooping juniper.

'Okay, Marcus, I get the picture!' he thought. There would be remounts. He could go hell for leather. 'Do your damndest, Whit!' Lucha had said. So he let the horse run. It went at a hard lope and he stood in the stirrups. A quarter-mile off he reined in, rifle raised, and studied the layout. No one lived here, that was clear, but was the owner of the horse inside the roofless jacal? This was *Round Corral*, he supposed. There was no smoke, no sign of men, only the horse watching him. He rode slowly in and circled the adobe at a respectable distance. Seeing nothing, he rode the sweating horse up to the corral.

He rode in, dismounted, and approached the horse, a dun with rough, strong lines. Who had left it here for him? The horse stood while he checked it over. Not bad. He carried the saddle and blanket to it and cinched up. He led both horses out and lifted the bars back into place, then he noticed a slip of paper under a rock on the corral wall as he mounted.

'Next horse at Joe Spring. Six miles.'

He shook the rifle. So long, Clane! *Adiós*, Father Clark. He could let the horse out now. He felt a pang of sorrow and guilt. And good-bye, Missy . . .

He led the gelding a couple of miles, traveling at a run, before he cut it loose. The dun gave a hard ride. It was cold-jawed but strong, Mexican-trained, used to having its head yanked around rather than being reined. It knew the trail because it had come up it, and since it was going home it would pull well all the way. He could see its hoof-tracks and those of the rider who had brought it here in the earth, clean-edged impressions only a day old.

He rode hard, still wondering who had brought horses here. Missy? Could she have dropped them off? No, she wouldn't have been horsewoman enough to lead three or four horses, nor would she have had the opportunity.

As he penetrated deeper into the canyons of the rough, towering walls of stone and shale, there was more growth along the trail—tough little junipers, Spanish oak, screwbean mesquite. Maguey clung to cracks in canyon walls, looking like giant green artichokes. He talked to the horse in Spanish, the feel of freedom like whiskey in him. The sun gleamed on yellow hillsides. He was hungry. He hoped Marcus had not forgotten food. It was a hundred and fifty miles home, maybe more, through an almost deserted country where sirloins did not grow on trees.

In an arroyo choked with mesquite and prickly pear, he came upon a clump of junipers. A fence made of thorny ocotillo wands woven together with wire formed a large, irregular corral: *Joe Spring Camp*. He was on someone's untamed, wide-open ranch, where now and then a few cattle or horses were curried out of the brakes and penned here for branding. A big horse with a Roman-nose, looking half trained and spooky, stood inside the thorny fence watching him approach. It had been tugging at a truss of wild hay.

Jackson saw a Mexican bridle hanging on the fence. He went inside, talking to the horse, took the bridle and walked toward the horse. Whit was breathing hard. The horse moved away.

'Now, then,' he said quietly. 'Stand easy, horse. Time's what I've got least of.'

There were no corners in a corral like this one. He would make one try, then ride the other horse in and do it mounted. But it stood, its hind legs to him, as he went up sweet-talking it.

He got it bridled, led the other horse in and switched the saddle. Using the reins, he led the used horse on down the arroyo.

*　　*　　*

At *Horse Camp* a blue roan was penned in a corral made of shale slabs. Branding irons hung from a limb of a madrone near a small adobe hut. The horse was small, but strong where it counted, with flat-boned pasterns and muscular legs. Horses had been penned here overnight, he decided. Probably the man who had dropped the animals at the various points had camped here one night. The horse wore a curlicued Mexican brand.

He made the remount and rode out, taking the Roman-nosed horse along for a mile. They would get no use out of the broncs he was finished with. He took the bridle with him when he turned the horse loose.

*　　*　　*

He realized he must be nearing the river, for there was a pattern to the mountains that suggested a drop-off just beyond them. The skyline was of camel humps, knobs, and notches. There were rocks and loose stone; the trail climbed, switching back and forth. The ground was red roan in color, and jays fussed in the Spanish oaks and juniper. The horse was breathing hard, and he prayed, *Don't give out!* and *Be there, horse,* as he worried about both present and future. Shadows were brimming in the canyons. Around a turn he came to a rock pen against a low cliff. His glance found scraps of old harness, a couple of feed sacks, and a horse waiting for him.

And on the dry-laid rock wall a blue bandana was spread out, pinned down by stones. Now, what did that mean? He studied it; there was no note with it. He shoved it in his pocket, glad to have it, but not understanding.

Miles back, he heard a rifle whang and echo. Had someone seen him? or was it a shot fired in frustration? A posseman killing one of his remounts that he couldn't catch? The horse had been browsing on a heap of blond-tasseled chino grass. The little canyon was all in shadow. According to his map, this was *Panther Spring*, and there were hoofprints everywhere. At this point the rider had had a string of four horses, plus his own mount. He was quite a horseman to have handled such a string, though Whit had seen the drag-marks of chain hobbles.

This was a bay horse, and a traveler, long-legged and deep in the barrel. Someone had figured, *About here he'll need a travelin' horse.* Another shot back in the crags! Make haste slowly, he told himself. He might be in a hurry, but the horse wasn't. He had to let the old bridle out a couple of notches for this long-headed brute.

'*¡Vámonos!*'

There was a climb and then suddenly a view of the river and of Mexico—of freedom!

Far below him was the green, shadowed river with its sandbars and brushy banks. Beyond it to the west, a sweep of land like an old wrinkled hide ran out to the horizon. There was a broken plateau under the rim, a valley running on down the river, with mesas like islands, and in the distance, pink in the evening light, a mountain range.

One more corral. One more horse!

It was somewhere below, just across the river according to the map. It would be almost dark before he found it near the wide, shallow Rio Grande that divided the two nations.

The trail tilted steeply down. The horse gave him a hard ride and was not sure-footed. A mule would have been a better choice. But the trail was clear enough, down little canyons in the mass of the cliffs, out along rocky hillsides. He saw a dust-puff on the trail a hundred feet ahead of him, then heard the echoing report of a rifle. Another. Then a scatter of shots too far off to worry about. They were miles behind by trail, but only a mile or so as the crow flies, and probably taking desperation shots at him.

A few hundred feet above the jungle of rocks and shrubs at the base of the cliffs, the horse slipped on a turn and went down on its side. Whit swore. He left the saddle on the high side, landed on his right hip and arm, raised his head and saw the animal go scrambling over the edge of the trail! He could hear it rolling over and over from ledge to ledge. Then it was quiet except for a rattle of small stones.

Dazed, he studied the river. It was a half-mile away by trail, at least. And then there would be the wide river to cross in the sunset, and the possemen coming fast behind him. He turned and studied the boulders and cliffs above. He had a choice: to hole up above the trail and hope to knock off all the possemen before they took cover, or to run for it and hope for the best. But he hadn't enough shells for a prolonged standoff, nor was he ready to see his picture on dead-or-alive posters.

Carrying the rifle, he started sliding down the cliffside.

CHAPTER SEVENTEEN

He found the dead horse among the rocks and stripped off the saddle. The tree was broken, but it was usable. Sweating and gasping, he managed to get the stirrup and cinch from under the horse. Then he scrambled on down the rocks toward the river.

Before he reached the bottom, he could see the posse above him, and a few more shots, less wild now, winged in. He slid down the last crumbling cliff to the stream bed. The river was a couple of hundred yards wide, shallow and ribbed by long sandbars like steamboat hulls. On the American side there was a tangle of boulders and brush. The Mexican side was more open, hardly ten feet above high-water, and with a few small trees near the river. There were thickets of pale-green cane.

Beyond, he saw a tiny jacal of brush and adobe a couple of hundred yards from the edge of the river, and an ocotillo-branch corral. Beyond that it was rough, rising ground running out to a range of dark hills. Night was closing in. If he made it across, and it became a chase, the darkness might save him.

He ran toward the river and splashed into the shallows. In a few yards it was up to his knees. He could hear distant whooping and the clatter of stones. The mud was ankle deep and slowed him. Burdened with the rifle and saddle, he struggled on, hearing the horsemen howling and swearing, yelling as though chasing wild cattle. He reached a sandbar and stumbled across to the next shallow channel of mossy water. He slashed through it to another sandbar, and just as he staggered from the water up a silted slope where scattered willows grew, he heard a shot from somewhere before him! It passed high over his head.

'¿Quién vive?' a man shouted.

Whit stopped dead. Logically, it must be the

61

man who had stationed the remounts. 'Whit Jackson!' he shouted back.

'*¿Apúrese, patrón!*'

Whit trotted forward, burdened by the broken saddle.

'Ramón?' he called.

'*A su servicio.*' A Mexican in a short black coat and leather trousers slipped from the crumbling adobe, a carbine in his hand. It was Ramón Arreola, who had worked for him part time for fifteen months, his only hired hand, but a hard-working one. Ramón pulled a latch from the willow-branch gate so that Whit could lug the saddle into the corral. Then he got busy emptying a Henry rifle into the cliff a half-mile away. The weapon roared and smoked.

Whit saddled in haste, surprised that Ramón had been the one to stake out the horses for him, a man who owed him little and himself had barely escaped prosecution in the frameup. He had a wife and five children on the Mexican side, but for months he had spent most of his time working for Whit, saving money to pay off a scrap of farmland across the Río Bravo del Sur.

As he fired, bursts of dust exploded before the possemen strung out along the trail. The horsemen were just above the tide of darkness lapping the cliff. As the slugs landed, the manhunters hastily pulled up and got busy making themselves hard to hit.

The horse in the corral was a big deep-chested roan. It was rough looking, but would probably carry well. '*¿Ya mero?*' Ramón called. He looked solemn and anxious, a man who took all things seriously.

'*¡Ya mero!*' Whit grinned at the Mexican. In his black coat and big *jipi* straw sombrero, a bandolier across his chest, he looked like a tintype of a Mexican revolutionary. Yet he was only a farmer.

*   *   *

A clearcut trail led into the hills. They rode hard for a while, then reined in and let the horses jog. 'Who sent you?' Whit asked Ramón.

'Señor St. Clair talked to me about it first. I said I was willing. He explained it all to me—but then he died. Everybody was very sad, and I was sad about you. But after the funeral, his daughter asked me if I would do it, and I said, Okay! So she got me the money, and gave me a map.

'I bought some horses at a ranch near here a couple of days ago. And I put them in the corrals yesterday, and left some food and a gun at a smuggler's camp not much farther now.'

'I'll pay you back, Ramón. I don't know when, and I don't know how, but I'll never forget.'

'*Si Dios quiere*,' said Ramón, piously.

'What do I do if I make it to San Felipe?'

'Señora Lucha said to wait there, across the river. When I bring word, someone will come.'

'Probably Billy Murphy! Isn't her husband the sheriff now?'

'Yes, but I don't think he's a gunfighter. I don't know what he'll do . . .'

Across from Los Lobos, San Felipe was on the Mexican side of the Río Bravo del Sur, the splinter of the Rio Grande that had formed fifteen years ago during the flood. Now it was a meager all-year stream running in the shape of a large noose below the Rio Grande.

'How long did it take you?' Whit asked.

'Two weeks on the way. And then a few days to learn the trail from the river to Terlingua, and to buy the horses.'

They rode steadily. Nighthawks darted across the trail, and there were the *cha-qua-ka!* calls of harlequin quail in the brush. It was almost dark. Whit was hungry, and would have liked a drink.

'I wonder how soon they'll know in Los Lobos that I've escaped?' he speculated.

'Soon. Didn't Señor St. Clair tell you? They have a telegraph line now.'

'I guess he forgot to tell me that,' said Whit ruefully. 'But what's the difference? The day I ride across the river, the wolves are going to howl.'

At the camp there was dried venison, beans

64

Ramón had boiled and mashed, and ceramic-hard tortillas he had been carrying for days. There was also tequila, and Whit drank it with the cold food and felt a little fire of warmth and relaxation begin in his belly. He wondered if he would ever see Missy again. And Rip Clane. He hoped Clane had not connected Missy's behavior with his own escape. Nor that Father Clark would suspect her of aiding him. He would make life hell for her.

CHAPTER EIGHTEEN

Whit bought a cheap, rawhide-covered saddle tree at a pueblo in the mountains. The saddlemaker fitted it to the torn hull of his saddle. Riding south, they killed rabbits with small-game cartridges Ramón had brought along, and bought goat meat from farmers. Sometimes they camped overnight at a primitive Mexican ranch in a wilderness of hills and barrancas.

On the tenth day, Ramón pointed east. 'That's a railroad—that smoke. The river splits there.'

By that night they were near the orphan river that had split off from the Big River. Bare cottonwoods, looking like smoke themselves, traced the bosque. They camped away from the river, for they were now in

Hatcher country. The old savage called Sam Hatcher, who claimed most of the basin between the two rivers, would be looking for him.

For Jackson had let the cat out of the bag— the suspicion that Hatcher did not own the basin at all, that he had merely appropriated it after it became American territory. That was why he had railroaded him to prison—to make an example of him. Yet now, as far as Whit knew, people still pretended to believe the fable that Hatcher, whom they had bought land from, was the rightful original owner.

*   *   *

Late the next day they saw the smoke of San Felipe in the dusk. There was a small earth dam upstream from the town; downstream there were trees and farms along the Mexican side, for the dam furnished enough water for irrigation. The American side was largely cattle country—too rough for more than a few farms like Billy and Lucha Murphy's.

As darkness fell, they rode into the village. Whit filled himself with its flavor. Everything was the same gray-brown color. There were gap-toothed streets formed by huts from which drifted the fragrance of charcoal fires. They reached the little church on its high foundation of stones, confronting a small plaza with dusty *palmitos*. In a few stores catering to

66

peasants there was lamplight. Horses stood at rails before two cantinas, and a couple of men stood outside a small restaurant.

On a corner was a one-story hotel, the Hacienda de San Felipe. Ramón reined in.

'Señora Murphy said for you to stay here. I'll take word to her.'

'And then you'd better forget about me for a while. I may draw flies, Ramón.'

'I'll be back, *patrón*,' Ramón insisted earnestly.

A boy came from an arched passage that led into the hotel. He took the horse, led it through the arch and across a courtyard to another passage. Inside the arch there was a door. Whit carried his roll of gear and his rifle into the manager's quarters.

A very stout man in cotton pants and a shirt without a collar emerged from an adjoining room. Whit remembered him and thought he must be doing well—he was getting fatter.

'*¿Qué tal*, Fiero?' he said. 'Have you got a room for me?'

'Certainly. All paid for.' The man opened a ledger at a desk and wrote Whit's name in a tangle of flourishes. 'The room with the blue door, around the corner to your left. Someone wanted me to let him know when you arrived.'

'Billy Murphy?'

'No, this man's name is Simms. I believe he bought your little ranch. He's staying in town. You see, señor, we knew you were coming.'

'I've heard. What do they say about it in the cantina?'

Fiero shrugged. 'Not much. But everyone is interested. One moment while I light you a candle.'

Carrying the candle, Whit found the small room around the corner, opening on the courtyard. It had an earth floor, a rope-sling cot, a stool on three legs, and a pitcher and basin on a bench. He washed up and dried his hands and face on his shirt-tail.

He was hungry, and there was no point in waiting here for Lucha or Simms. Either might come in an hour or two, or not until tomorrow. He walked down the street to the restaurant he had seen. There were a half-dozen small tables, and through a doorway he could see a woman stirring a kettle of beans at a bracero stove. At the moment there were no customers.

He sat down facing the door, and leaned his rifle against the wall. He felt edgy. He had known the feeling of freedom and of being a prisoner, and now he was getting the feeling of being hunted. The proprietor came, and Whit asked for a bottle of tequila and for some *machaca*, beans, and tortillas.

A couple of Mexicans entered, courteously tipped their hats, and sat down.

Whit thought about John Simms.

It was strange that Simms would be backing out now, if he had felt confident enough to buy

Jackson's ranch from Sam Hatcher, or to accept it as payment for some favor.

What favor could Simms have done Hatcher?

The former had come to the ranch one day, a year after Whit filed on it and defied Hatcher to throw him off. Simms brought a team of Engineer surveyors and a couple of cavalrymen. He said he was looking for certain monuments left by Mexican or Spanish surveyors. He had found nothing, as far as Whit knew, and he and his men had departed.

Not long after that, Whit was arrested for stealing LLCC horses. And now Simms was on the spread, and wanted to talk to Whit . . .

He went back to the hotel. With the curtain drawn, he lay resting on the cot, his rifle beside him, until a knock came on the door.

CHAPTER NINETEEN

Whit stood at one side of the door and called, *'¿Quién es?'*

'John Simms,' a voice said with false heartiness.

Carefully he opened the door. The candlelight fell on a tall man with a stomach like a sack of meal, supported from beneath by a broad belt. He held a gray Stetson in one hand, and his face was florid and sheepish. His thin, dark hair was brushed sidewise across a bald scalp. Whit barely recalled him. His mouth was partly open in a kind of loose grin, and the younger man could smell whiskey on him. Now that he was out of uniform, the ex-lieutenant seemed totally devoid of authority.

'I guess you're Whit Jackson, eh?' he said. 'I think we've met—'

'I've changed, and I'd say you had, too.'

'*Correcto*,' said Simms heartily. 'Say, I suppose you know Sam Hatcher let me stay on that land you were—er—using. So what I came to say—Can I come inside?'

'This is fine.'

'Sure. Suit yourself. I just thought—' Simms glanced back. 'I brought your horse and saddle,' he said.

''Dobe? That's a good horse. What about the others?'

'Some of them are still there. I haven't done much with the place. It was just a place to stay while—I'm really working for Sam Hatcher—running lines for fences and all. And a ditch, maybe.'

'You finished up the boundary stuff before I left, I think. So all the official boys have gone home?'

'Yup!' Simms put his hat on. 'And me, I'm packed and ready to go. Packed and ready to go,' he repeated. 'Any time you want to come back.'

'But it's not your land, you say?'

'No, no. I was just camping there. Still the property of Double L Double C. Do you want to look at the horse?'

'I want to look at you, first.' Whit held the candle close to his face, without leaving the doorway. Simms appeared nervous and embarrassed. Whit blew out the candle. 'Okay, let's take a look. Where did you leave the horse?'

'In the *zaguán*.'

'Bring it here.'

Simms walked around the corner into the passageway and reappeared leading a horse. It was a large buckskin, with familiar lines. Carrying the rifle, Whit ran one hand over its forelegs and patted its withers. He placed his hand on its ribs.

'What have you fed him—scraps?' he asked.

'We didn't have a lot of rain last summer. Hardly made a stand of grass.'

'That's when you buy hay. Okay, I'll take care of it. *Adiós*.'

'Any idea when you'll be wanting to move in?'

'None at all,' Whit said.

Simms nodded. Then: 'Listen, I wanted to say—well, I know it must have been pretty rough up there. But I didn't have anything to do with—' He faltered.

'With what?'

'With him charging you. I was gone before that ever happened.'

71

'Then how did you happen to come back?'

Simms made a faltering gesture. 'The old man wrote me. Did I want to have the use of your place, and what I could make on the horses, in return for running some fence lines? I was fed up with the Army right then, and I said okay. Now, I doubt whether it made sense. Any sense at all. I'm no rancher. Think I'll go back into the Army. I've still got my commission.'

Whit looked at him blankly. Finally Simms nodded. 'So, that's it!'

'Maybe you can tell me something.'

'What's that?'

'Is Kramer still around?'

'Kramer?'

'He was a horsebreaker for Hatcher. A big man, looked a little Indian. He was the main witness against me.'

Simms pulled his hat brim down so that his face was nearly obscured. 'I think I've seen him around.'

'Tell him I'll be looking him up.'

'All right. But—'

'Yeah?'

'Well, do you know what you're going to do?'

'No. But I'll think of something. We had a lot of time to make up stories and things in Terlingua.'

*   *   *

Whit moved the cot to block the door when eleven o'clock came and no one else arrived. With the bench it made a neat wedge between door and wall, so that no one could break in on him. He slept lightly.

CHAPTER TWENTY

He was in the restaurant having breakfast among shopkeepers when a dapper, spruce-looking Mexican dressed in a black suit came in from the street and looked over the room. Whit knew at once that the man was looking for him. He had keen gray eyes, a somber face, down-curving mustaches, and long sideburns. On his lapel he wore a silver star. The man saw Whit and came to his table. Whit did not pick up his rifle, but he was prepared to deal with the man if he made a move to arrest him.

He would have to work it out about the other side of the river, but here he was not yet jail bait.

'Señor Jackson?' the lawman said. 'Venancio Aguirre, at your service.'

Whit rose cautiously and offered his left hand. He saw no one in the street who appeared to be backing up the sheriff's play. 'Sit down, Marshal. Have a cup of coffee.'

'No coffee, thank you. But I'll sit down.'

73

He was wearing a gun but rather pointedly kept his hands on the table. 'Did you have a good trip from Terlingua?'

Whit made a rocking motion with his fist, two fingers extended like horns. *'Así así.'*

'Arreola is a good man. He took a big risk for you.'

'I'm at his service. What can I do for you?'

'I want to explain my position. I am charged with keeping the peace in San Felipe. If you were Mexican, I would have to arrest you. I understand that you are an outlaw, but since you are an American, I don't have to arrest you.'

'Bien, bien.'

'But Sheriff Murphy, across the river, has told me that there is pressure on him to ask for your extradition. If that happens, and the authorities ask me to deliver you to him, then I will have to do it. But I will give you twenty-four hours warning if it should happen.'

'My lawyer told me that my crime is not an extraditable offense. And I'm not an outlaw, just a man on the dodge.'

'Fine. I regret the whole business. Over there, you have Mr. Sam Hatcher, who runs things. Here we have General Lopez y Durán. He is an honorable man, unlike some. He sold the land along the river to the farmers who now live there. Their titles are secure. As it happens, he is nearby, at his hacienda near town. Well, I wish you good health, señor. If I

74

can help—'

'Is there a gun shop in San Felipe now?'

'Yes, on the plaza. Hardware and other items. And I own the saddle shop. *A su servicio.*'

Whit was tired of lugging Rip Clane's rifle everywhere he went. He picked out a second-hand Colt revolver at the hardware store, and went up the street to the saddle shop and bought a belt and holster from Aguirre. He had never packed a revolver, and it was like carrying a hammer on his hip. He left the rifle in his room and went to the office.

'Has anybody been looking for me?'

'The *jerife*, señor, I regret to say.'

'The American *jerife*?'

'No, Sheriff Aguirre.'

'We've had a talk, Fiero. Will you have the boy get my horse? The buckskin?'

In a few minutes the boy led his horse into the *zaguán*, and he walked it out to the plaza, mounted, and gazed around, testing the stubble on his cheeks. He was not going anywhere, but he felt crippled without a horse under him, or one waiting nearby. There was a quiet traffic of wagons, horses, and pedestrians to and from the shops and the church in the middle of the plaza. He rode up the street, looking at the shops and the people, especially the people. He saw no Americans. Then he spotted a barber shop, and went inside. There were two chairs, one barber, and three or four empty waiting chairs. The barber, a big man with a handsome mustache, was stropping a razor near a washstand.

'Yes, sir!' he said.

Whit took the chair in the rear. After the barber pinned an apron around his neck, Whit eased the Colt from the holster and laid it in his lap.

The barber cut his hair. 'A shave?' he asked afterward.

'Everything, my friend.'

He was fully lathered when Lucha Murphy appeared in the doorway. She looked excited and beautiful in a blue-and-white gown, her dark hair pinned up. She was carrying a red leather portfolio that Whit recognized as her father's. 'Whit?' she said.

'Made it!' Whit said, grinning through the lather.

She came to him and laid her hands on his shoulders. There was moisture in her eyes. 'So glad!' she said. 'Now we'll show them!'

Whit reached out and clasped her hand. Then he saw a man come into the doorway. He freed his hand and sought the Colt. The other was a big, grinning man with curly black hair, sparkling eyes, and the exuberance of a lunatic.

'Hey, you old outlaw!' he bellowed. 'Gotcha!' He faked a pass at the gun he was wearing but did not draw it. He wore a sheriff's badge that in no way went with his slightly mad expression.

'I'd argue that with you if I didn't have a razor at my throat,' Whit said. 'Go ahead, barber, before the soap dries.' The barber began trimming his side-burns, his hand trembling slightly. Whit realized that barbers knew more about the local gossip than anyone.

'Well, how about this coon!' Murphy said, sitting down, gripping his knees, and staring at Jackson. 'You son of a gun! You made it.'

Lucha moved away and sat down with the portfolio on her lap. It was clear that she was troubled.

'It was simple. They turned their back on me one day.' He did not know whether Billy Murphy knew about his wife's part in the jailbreak or not. 'Two hoots and I was gone.'

'You heard about your lawyer?' Murphy said. 'My daddy-in-law? He died in his sleep. Not a bad way to go, when your time comes.'

Lucha said, 'I've more or less taken over the work he had in progress. I got my license to practice, you know.'

Billy Murphy beat his knees with his fists. 'Isn't that a laugh? A she-lawyer in a mudhole like Los Lobos?' Then: 'Hey, listen, *amigo*! It looks like you may be a lifelong citizen of Mexico now, so what you're going to need is a bucket of Spanish gold pieces. And I happen to know where they're at.'

'What are you talking about?'

'Spanish treasure!' Murphy said, his eyes

77

burning. 'I met this Mexican army officer while I was fighting in Puebla. I took a bullet in the thigh there, but that's another story. He told me about this old Spanish mission in the state of Sonora where there's a treasure buried!—'

'Oh, Billy,' Lucha sighed. 'We're talking serious business.'

'So am I, and shut up. You see, Whit, the missions were run by the church, but the money they made was supposed to be sent back to the king. You follow? Well, this particular mission is in the Yaqui country, and they were digging gold till hell wouldn't have it! But they were keeping it. So the king sent some troops and asked for his gold. But all they gave him was a few hundred ounces. The rest—'

'Is buried under the altar?' Whit asked wryly.

'It's damn sure buried somewhere. I'm trying to get a couple of other men to throw in with me, to go over there and—'

'That's a thousand miles, Billy, and the Yaquis are perpetually on the warpath,' Lucha said. 'And it'll be planting time soon, and we can't leave the farm to the hired hands to run for us. You've got a deputy now, so you'll just have to take time off and start the plowing.'

'A deputy!' Whit said. 'Things must be moving faster in Los Lobos. Anybody I know?'

'Oh, yes,' Lucha said archly. 'I don't know whether it's a joke or what. But at Sam

78

Hatcher's insistence, Billy deputized Hank Kramer last week. He's turned into a sot since you left, and just about the only work Billy has is locking him up after a drunken fight every week. And now he's a deputy!'

'Oh, for sweet Susanna's sake,' Murphy muttered. 'A man walks under a whiskey sign and Lucha claims he's drunk. Kramer—well, I've got to serve some papers on people that haven't kept up their interest payments to Hatcher on land they bought. Sam has a good point. If an ugly animal like Hank walks in and suggests that they get it up, there ain't going to be any argument.'

'Where were we?' Whit asked.

Murphy looked him in the eye at last.

'I'll tell you where you are, Whit,' he said. 'And I think you may decide a treasure hunt on the Pacific Coast ain't a bad idea. The State of Texas has asked for extradition papers on you. If it goes through, I'll have to arrest you.'

'Mexico will not extradite a person for horsetheft,' said his wife. 'Especially when the case is being appealed.'

'*Still?*' Murphy exclaimed.

'Yes, and with a date set for a hearing.'

The barber finished and wiped Jackson's face with a damp towel. 'Are you my friend, Billy?' Whit asked.

'Of course. What do you need?'

'Then why did you let Hatcher force Kramer on you?'

Murphy glanced out the door, then shrugged. 'Well, if it comes to arresting you, I don't want to have to do it myself.'

The barber removed the apron, and there it was, glinting in the light—Jackson's revolver pointing at the sheriff.

'Nobody's going to arrest me, Billy,' Whit said. 'I'm not going back to prison—that's the first thing to understand. Once you understand that, you can see there's a lot of pressure on everybody involved in this. Especially on Kramer. Hatcher appointed him hoping he and I would have a showdown. I'm going to have a talk with him, and he's going to tell me how much it cost Hatcher to frame me with those horses. And before I'm through, he's going to be testifying for me, and against Hatcher.'

'Put it away,' Murphy said, scowling at the Colt. 'I told you I couldn't arrest you. I think you better settle down and appreciate the advice people are giving you.'

'Oh, have you got some advice for me?'

Murphy stood up. 'Yes—as a matter of fact. Stay out of town. In a nut shell.'

'It's the right nut in the wrong shell, Billy,' Lucha said briskly. 'Do you want to know something? Something that will take Los Lobos and shake it upside down like a sack? You aren't a sheriff at all.'

'Oh, I ain't? This ain't gravy on my coat, it's a badge.'

80

'The whole story is in my portfolio. You aren't a lawman, and Hatcher doesn't own any land, and neither does anybody in Knox County! And I'm going to explain it all at a meeting tomorrow.'

Murphy clenched her wrist. 'You are like hell! You're going back to the farm today and tend to your knitting. Being a so-called lawyer has addled your brains.'

'Whit, I'll just tell you this now,' Lucha said. 'My father was onto something big when he told you long ago that the Los Lobos Land and Cattle Company didn't own *anything*, and that you could claim a section of land under the Homestead Act. But he wasn't quite clear on it then. Now the work is finished, and the last time he was in Austin he asked for another international boundary commission to inquire into it.

'Because the land was never legally acquired from Mexico after the river divided! It's still Mexican! It belongs to General Lopez y Durán!'

'Shut up!' Murphy backhanded her across the mouth. '*I thought I told you!*—'

Whit was out of the chair, jamming his Colt away, and seizing Murphy from behind. He shoved him into a corner and yanked his gun from the holster. Then he let him go, and as Murphy turned he gave him a quick chop to the chin. Murphy's eyes glazed, and he slumped to the floor. Whit took the barber's

81

wash-basin from the table and hurled the soapy water onto his head.

In a moment Murphy rubbed his forehead and began to come to. Whit helped him up, led him to the door, and shoved him out into the street. Though he was furious, his mounting passion was for what Lucha had just said.

Whit turned back and saw her touching a cut on her swollen upper lip. Sitting beside her, he took the towel the barber handed him. 'Oh, listen!' he said in anguish. 'Why did you ever do it?'

'Marry Billy? The usual reason.'

'Do you still love him?'

'It doesn't really matter. Whit, dear, listen to me. I want you to stay in San Felipe for a while and—and just be careful. I'm going to drive out and talk to General Lopez at his hacienda now. He promised to be at that meeting I mentioned. But I'd rather you didn't come, even though legally no one has a right to try to arrest you in Los Lobos. You see, everyone in the county is affected, and people are going to be frightened and probably angry.'

'Are you sure about this boundary thing?'

'There's simply no question! The boundary commission didn't finish its work. The old monuments remain in effect. The Rio Grande is the international boundary.'

He filled his lungs and gazed out the door. He saw Murphy riding away. 'So if somebody tried to arrest me—'

'You'd be just as dead if you resisted and got shot. Stay here. I'll stay with the Lopez family tonight. As a matter of fact,' she said, 'I don't really expect to be the best-loved person in Los Lobos myself after tomorrow!'

CHAPTER TWENTY-ONE

Ramón was waiting at the hotel. His horse was at the hitch-rack, and he squatted on the walk with his back against the sun-warmed adobe wall. He looked at Whit's arsenal, the rifle and the Colt, and smiled.

'Well, you look like a real outlaw now.'

'I am a real one. Billy Murphy was just telling me not to cross the river.'

'I saw Sheriff Murphy riding by without his wife. And I've talked to Señor Hatcher this morning. He wants to talk to you.'

'A lot of people do. And I want to talk to him, when I'm ready.'

'Let's go inside, patrón,' Ramón said.

In the tiny bedroom, Whit sat on the cot, the Mexican in the chair. Whit had barred the door. 'Now, then.'

'He wants to meet you, tonight, on this side of the river.'

'Where?'

'At the old álamo tree near the dam. He'll

build a fire there so you can see him. You'll come and talk to him, alone. He promises he won't carry a gun. I told him I'd talk to you and take back word.'

'Tell him I'll come if I can bring you, too. Are you willing?'

'Do you trust him?'

'No. That's why I want you along.'

'I'll tell him, then.'

Whit spent the day making plans for his horse ranch. There were ten or twelve acres of good level land near the river, and he wondered whether he could make an alfalfa crop on it. Lucha had worked out a system of irrigation for the farm Billy Murphy had been fooling around with when she married him, and it functioned very well. Maybe she could engineer some ditches for him, too. Harvesting might be a problem, but there was plenty of willing Mexican labor around.

Now, of course, there was the new problem of his not owning that land!

But the problem was partially offset by the fact that everything that had happened to him no longer counted, legally. He was not a convict. He had no record. He had been jailed and tried illegally.

And there were things about the Los Lobos Basin that only a lawyer, and perhaps an international survey commission, could settle, things that would involve every rancher, farmer and businessman between the Río

84

Bravo del Sur and the Rio Grande.

And because of those matters, Sam Hatcher, that old wolf of the Rio Grande, wanted to talk to him.

Ramón returned in mid-afternoon.

'He'll meet us. But he says that if there's going to be two of us, he'll carry a gun.'

'He'd have carried a derringer anyway. What time?'

'Eight o'clock.'

They rode through the dark brush, avoiding the river road, which was a potential ambuscade. It was over a mile to the big, leafless cottonwood near the river. The horses scuffed along over the silty soil. The cold dry air bit at their faces like a fox. At last Whit saw a tiny flake of orange light, and reined in. He dismounted and handed his reins to Ramón. He told him what to do, and the Mexican walked the horses ahead.

Whit went on, carefully, his Colt drawn but uncocked. The earth was level and bare. As he walked, he stopped now and then to peer ahead. The ember of light grew until it was a flicker; then he could see a man seated near it. He went on, picking his way like an Indian. At last he saw what he had known would be there.

A man was lying on the ground before him, his hat beside him. His cheek was pressed against the stock of a rifle.

Whit stood silently. He could not yet make out Ramón and the horses, but the clop of hoofs was audible. He studied the rolling land all around. It was too dark to determine whether other men were covering the camp. Finally he decided to take this one and then look for others.

Ramón was approaching the campfire. The gunman raised his head and shoulders, like a lizard. His attention was focused entirely on the horsemen who were drawing near, as Whit went toward him in a crouch. He could make out wide, craggy shoulders, thick black hair, long legs. He remembered Hank Kramer on the stand denying that he had ever joined Whit and Ramón on the trail near Fort Collins with a herd of horses.

'No, sir. I was breaking horses at a horse pasture called Comanche Head.'

Behind him now, Whit rested one hand on the ground as he raised the Colt. He chopped it down, and Kramer convulsed and lay clawing at the ground. Whit removed the man's gunbelt, then his belt, and made his hands fast behind him.

He took his guns and boots and carried them with him as he went on, leaving them finally by a bush. He studied the ground all about. He could see Ramón on the road fifty feet from the fire. And Sam Hatcher's head was raised as he watched the horse and rider come.

Whit moved off to the left on a big circle around the fire. Any other men on watch would probably be along the perimeter of that circle. But he did not think he would find any. It was the kind of job one man could handle, and there would be fewer witnesses. Witnesses were already becoming a nuisance to the old devil.

Voices, then. *'¿Quién vive?'*

'Ramón.'

'Well, where the hell is Jackson? Ain't that saddle empty?'

'He's coming. He stopped to relieve himself.'

'You're a liar. Keep coming. I've got you covered, greaser. I'll keep you covered till I see him.'

'Here I am,' Whit called, walking boldly toward the fire but still using all his senses.

Ramón sat in the saddle, holding the reins of the buckskin, when Whit walked into the light of the small mesquite-root fire. Hatcher stood beside it with a rifle. He was a lean, wolfish figure.

'Couldn't hold it, eh?' he jeered.

Holding the Colt in his hand, Jackson said: 'Maybe we'd better put the hardware away before somebody has an accident. And there's two of us and one of you, so—'

The rancher carefully laid the rifle on the earth, watching Whit holster his Colt.

Whit joined him at the fire, but Ramón sat his horse and watched. Hatcher took off his hat and pulled a folded paper from it. He was

87

nearly bald, with wrinkles in the scalp, wrinkles around his eyes, and deep lines beside his nose and mouth, the hard carvings of time and character. He was unshaven, had coarse black eyebrows, and large ears. There was a knife scar across the fleshy part of his nose.

'Reckon this will interest you,' he said, unfolding the paper. He held it so that Jackson could see the word *"Wanted."* 'A feller from Terlingua rode in with this yesterday,' he said. 'Made almost as good time as you did. He looked a little beat up, and wanted a job. His name is Clane. Not a very keen man, but I hired him for the calving time.'

'You're right, he's a little on the dull side. But he can do a simple job.'

Hatcher raised his arm to replace his Stetson, making a sweeping gesture as he settled it over his eyes. But just in case there were other men than Kramer, Whit stood close to Hatcher, to make a hazardous target.

Hatcher's coarse features looked tense as the seconds passed. 'Let's sit down,' Whit suggested. The rancher shrugged and sat down crosslegged. Whit sat down, too.

'What was it you had in mind?' he asked.

'I want to know what the hell you think you're going to do. You're outnumbered, outvoted, and unwanted. The State'll pay five hundred dollars for you, and I know a lot of men that'd kill you for less than that.'

Keep talking! Whit thought, a grim glee

rising like a bubble through him. Give Kramer time to sneak up on me.

'John Simms seems to think I may have a case,' he said. 'He offered me my ranch back last night. That's my horse I'm riding, and my saddle, if you doubt it.'

'Simms has changed his mind. He told me he was going to join the Army again. I told him I couldn't do without him. Talked him into staying.'

'Is he alive?'

Hatcher laughed. 'Oh, sure. Just a mite drunk.'

'Have you talked to Billy Murphy today?' Whit asked.

Hatcher chuckled. His voice had the texture of burlap. 'Billy's going to have to learn how to handle that wife of his. She's taken with some form of female craziness.'

'Maybe she's right.'

'About what?' asked the rancher. He moved a little nervously, as though a pebble under his rump bothered him. But he was cool, considering that by now he must suspect that something had gone wrong.

'Do I have to tell you?' Whit said. 'You came here twenty years ago. You and Colonel Ed scared the Mexicans out and passed the story around that the U.S. had bought the basin. That's why the colonel had to be cut in—to make a show of force with his horse cavalry.'

'You're as crazy as Murphy's wife!' the rancher shouted. 'It's all written in the records. It's U.S. land, and I bought it. There wasn't two dozen Mexicans in the whole basin and I paid them for what they used to own. There was more Comanches around than Mexicans, and I cleared this basin of the Comanche evil. And then some son of a bitch comes along and says, "I claim this section of land in the name of Whit Jackson." Well, the hell you do!' And he stole a quick glance up the slope behind Whit.

Whit picked up a twig and chewed on it, grinning. 'You're getting senile, Sam. There's no record of such a payment to the U.S. So the land still belongs to Lopez y Durán! Everybody will have to make his deal with him, even you!'

'You lost your brains up there, Jackson. I had Simms resurvey everything after you made your claim, and he said it was all tighter'n a tick.'

'Oh, no! You had Simms pussyfoot around, hoping to scare me off. When I didn't scare, then you hired Kramer and that other fellow to frame me. How's Kramer doing, by the way? Simms said he was still around. I thought he'd probably take off as soon as he heard I'd escaped.'

Hatcher gazed at him steadily.

'Wave your hat again,' Whit said. And he laughed.

Hatcher got to his feet. 'All right, I'll make you an offer. It's the last one you'll ever hear from me. Two thousand dollars—I've got it right here, in gold. If you agree to take off and never come back.'

'Make it fifty thousand and we've got a deal.'

Hatcher pointed at him. 'You'd better not cross the river, tomorrow or any time! If Clane don't get you, Murphy will. If he don't, I will.'

He leaned over the rifle. 'Leave it,' Whit said, drawing his Colt.

Hatcher said bitterly, 'Your word ain't worth a nickel any more, is it?'

'Not when a man makes a deal with me and sets a gunman in the brush to kill me. Where'd you leave your horse?'

'By the river.'

'Lead the way.'

He followed him to the bosque, where they came upon a horse standing tied to a mesquite. There was a musty smell of damp earth and rotting leaves. Hatcher mounted and waited.

'There's been times when I would have killed you, with a chance like this,' Whit said. 'I don't know why I don't. Maybe it goes against the grain. Maybe I want to see you wiped out. I'm going to buy all of your land that I can. And I won't be the only one. There's going to be a land rush.'

'What you don't know about men is that

91

most of them will run if you flap a horse blanket at them,' Hatcher scoffed. 'What you don't know about me is that I forgot how to quit, sometime or other. When I came here, I had to sleep on the ground with sticks under me so nobody would come up on me asleep. A country like this needs a bull of the woods, and I'm it. If you're going to kill me, Jackson, you better do it now.'

He was safe saying that, because he knew it went against Jackson's grain, that Jackson couldn't kill in cold blood.

'Two men that don't know each other,' Whit said. 'You don't seem to realize that I can't quit either. I'd still be coughing up red dust in Terlingua, if I could. Kramer won't be coming back, so don't wait around.'

*   *   *

Sheriff Aguirre was just locking up when they rode in. Hank Kramer, partially conscious, was tied across his horse as they pulled up. They had removed the saddle and left it in the brush.

'I charge this man with attempted murder,' Whit told the sheriff. Aguirre stood with his hand still on the doorknob. The jail was a small adobe-block building with a single barred window.

'That is a very serious charge,' Aguirre said.

'I have a witness—a Mexican citizen of good

repute.'

'I witnessed this crime,' said Ramón.

'We'll fill out the papers tomorrow if necessary,' said Whit. 'Maybe a doctor should check him out. I had to hit him on the head to disarm him. Here are the weapons he was carrying. Also his boots, which I took off so he couldn't escape. We'll help you get him settled. He's not walking very well.'

CHAPTER TWENTY-TWO

As he was eating breakfast at the restaurant, Ramón opened the door and glanced around until he saw Jackson in a corner with his back to the wall. 'Good morning, boss,' he said, drawing up a chair and calling to the child-waitress. *'Café tinto.'*

It was ten o'clock. Whit had walked the town, getting the feel and smell of it, and glancing across the river now and then at Los Lobos, which looked as quiet as ever.

'Very many people at the saloon,' said Ramón.

'Getting ready for a lynching?'

'Nobody talking much about you. Everybody's worried about the land thing. Have you heard?'

'I was there when Lucha Murphy sprang it on her husband. It's all General Lopez's—the whole county! Always has been. Just a bluff of Hatcher and Drum's.'

'*Ay que mujer,*' chuckled Ramón. 'That woman really a lawyer?'

'She's a lawyer. She was doing half her father's work when he died. She's quite a woman . . .'

Ramón glanced at him but said nothing.

'What are they saying?'

'Oh—you know. Some of them want to fight with guns. Nobody'll ever take it away from them. Most of them say it isn't true. But they're all going to the meeting.'

Whit leaned back against the wall. 'So am I.'

Ramón squinted at his coffee, his head on the side. 'I don't know, boss. It's your business, but—'

'The longer I put it off, the braver people are going to get. If Clane tries to take me, I'll kill him. And Clane knows it. Murphy won't try it, and Kramer can't. As for the rest of them, they aren't gunfighters, and most of them were my friends. So I plan on going to the meeting and then going out to the horse ranch. I figure matters will develop kind of naturally after that.'

'You sure got *cojones*,' said Ramón.

'And a lot of bug bites and bad memories. Nobody's taking me back, and I'm going to look them right in the eye at the meeting, and I think they'll get the point. Señorita?'

He beckoned the little waitress, paid his bill

with a gold peso piece and received in change some big copper and silver coins. He told Ramón, 'I'm going out to the ranch after the meeting. You might as well stay here till I come for you.'

'As you say, *patrón*. The meeting is set for noon.'

*   *   *

Whit walked over to the plaza and sought Aguirre's saddle shop. The sheriff was working on a bridle. Saddles rested on stands about the room, and there was a strong smell of Mexican leather. They shook hands.

'How's your prisoner doing?' he asked.

Aguirre grunted. '*Muy maltrecho*. He asks for liquor.'

'When he wants it badly enough, he'll tell the truth. He tried to ambush me last night. Has he told you about that?'

'He says *he* was ambushed.'

'He's lying. Sheriff, I need a Mexican flag. Can you find me one? You have one at the jail, don't you?'

'Yes. Behind my desk, on the wall.'

'I'd like to borrow it for a few hours.'

Aguirre tapped a leather-working tool with a wooden hammer. 'Will you bring it back without bullet holes?'

'I'll try.'

The small schoolhouse, a single room with two privies behind it, stood on a corner a block south of the main street of Los Lobos. Whit crossed the river below the bridge and reached the school by a back street. But the school was closed and padlocked. Was it Saturday? He had not reacquired the habit of keeping track of the days.

He tethered his horse in the rear and sat on the porch to wait. In a short time a buggy arrived, driven by a deep-chested, hearty old man with a white beard. He wore a fine gray suit with black braid on the lapels, and Whit knew it was General Lopez y Durán. Lucha rode beside him.

He stepped down to take the horse by the bridle. Lucha exclaimed in vexation, 'Why did you come?'

'I thought you might need this—' From a pocket Whit pulled a folded flag and shook it out.

'I don't know—it might add fuel to the flames,' she said.

'On the other hand, it might help them to believe what you're going to tell them. General,' he said to the Mexican, 'didn't you know about this all the time?'

The old man chuckled. 'Of course. But I wasn't using much of the land, and, after all, one does not argue with the United States cavalry.'

Lucha said hastily: 'There comes Tom Riordan! We'd better get inside.'

*   *   *

When Riordan, the owner of the livery stable, arrived with three other men, the flag had been thumb-tacked to the blackboard behind the teacher's desk. The room smelled of chalk dust and mesquite smoke. Lucha sat at the teacher's desk with her portfolio before her. At her left sat Whit, at her other side the general.

'Make yourselves comfortable, gentlemen,' she said. 'The desks and chairs are a bit small, but . . .'

Riordan took a small chair with a little table before it. The other men were Roy Farmer, a very tall old man who ranched near Whit; a sad-eyed man named Wendell Hill, another rancher; and Stu Perry, the furniture maker and undertaker.

'What's this all about, Lucha?' asked Perry, a formal-looking man with a shining red face.

'Let's wait till the others are here, so I'll only have to say it once,' said Lucha. 'You all know Whit Jackson, and this is General Lopez y Durán.'

Embarrassed, the men muttered acknowledgment and stole glances, from time to time, at Whit, the general, and the Mexican flag. Other men and a few women arrived, and the room began to fill. Zachary Lord, the mayor, sat in a corner seat with his jaw set. Whit had expected Billy Murphy to be on hand, but by the time Lucha opened the meeting he had not appeared. At last she stood up.

'Thank you for coming,' she said gravely. 'I hope everyone understands that we aren't here to upset or threaten anyone. We just want you to understand some very important things, and to clarify—certain matters.

'In a way, this is a memorial meeting for my father. He did most of the work and planning behind what I'm going to tell you. He enlisted General Lopez's cooperation in—in straightening things out.'

'Straightening what out?' Riordan called. 'Get to it!'

'All right, let's get to it,' Lucha said. 'Some of the rumors you've been hearing are crazy, but some are pretty close to the truth. The truth, friends—' She seemed to have to take a breath, and glanced briefly at Whit, as for reassurance.

'The truth is that Los Lobos, and Knox County, are part of Mexico. None of us owns an acre of American soil!'

Mayor Zachary Lord stood up. 'Yes, that's what we've been hearing, all right! But I don't believe it! How could it happen?'

'It happened because of a conspiracy. You

all know about the big rain, and the little Río Bravo del Sur—our river—splitting off and winding southwest down an old barranca. It didn't stop until it had captured over a half-million acres, and cut back to the Big River.'

She hesitated as a sound of horses came across a vacant lot from the main street. People stirred.

'Now,' Lucha continued, 'the question is, how did it get to be United States land? Well, an international survey commission came out, under an Army officer named Colonel Ed Drum, and a Mexican officer with some surveyors of his own, and they drew some lines and set up some concrete monuments.

'Then some congressmen talked, and suggested figures to the Mexicans for the purchase of the land. But nothing was ever agreed upon! Then Colonel Drum came back with some cavalrymen and chased out a little band of Indians and a few goat ranchers.'

The horsemen were before the schoolhouse. 'I'll wait until our late arrivals come in,' Lucha said.

They entered, looking fierce and angry, red-faced and embarrassed, or coarse and slightly drunk. Sam Hatcher was the fierce one, and he stopped and stared around the room with his head lowered and his hat brim pulled down. Under his own hat, lying on his lap, Whit gripped the secondhand Colt.

He had little idea of what was going to

happen. Few of the men in the schoolroom wore guns; they were not gun-toters, just ranchers, farmers, businessmen, and their wives. Behind Hatcher came John Simms—in uniform again—Billy Murphy with his star in plain sight, and Rip Clane.

'I got your invitation, Miz Murphy,' said Hatcher. 'I've watched cockfights, nigger-fights, and gun-fights, but I wouldn't miss this one for a pair of round dice.'

He scorned the children's seats and desks, and went to lean against the wall near a tintype of Sam Houston. Clane squatted down near him, John Simms took a chair, and Billy Murphy strode to the front.

'Lucha, I came to take you home,' he said brusquely.

'That was thoughtful of you, Billy. As soon as I'm through you can escort me to Father's office.'

'You don't seem to get the point!—'

'Sit down, Billy,' Whit said. 'You aren't in Texas now—you're in Mexico.'

'And that is the whole Goddamned *point*!' Murphy shouted.

'Don't do anything you'll be ashamed of, Billy,' Lucha said quietly. 'Any disturbance is *liable* to end in violence, and I promise you anyone who attempts to stop this meeting will end up in a Mexican jail.

'Now, then—' She turned to the map on the wall. With a pointer, she traced the course of the Rio Grande. 'That's the old United States border. And it also happens to be the present one. Because other than Colonel Drum's chasing out the original settlers, a few goat ranchers and farmers, nothing ever happened to change the boundary!'

Men were leaning forward, hands clutching papers or simply linked together; women gasped and glanced at each other.

'The most formal thing that ever happened was that a man named Sam Hatcher, who says he fought with Sam Houston and bought the Los Lobos Basin from the State of Texas, who had annexed it—he claimed the whole area and began selling parcels! How many of you bought land from Los Lobos Land and Cattle Company?'

Nearly every man raised his hand, many of them waving official-looking papers. Riordan, the livery-man, stood up. 'I bought mine from Ethan King, who bought his from somebody else—'

'All titles,' Lucha said, 'going back to what Sam Hatcher claims is his original deed. They're all trash, all worthless!'

'I didn't buy any,' Whit spoke up. 'I never did like the smell of this thing after I talked to Colonel Drum—before he sold out to Hatcher and left a few years ago. So I hired your daddy to research it for me, and he said it was all a— a hurrah's nest, I think he called it. So I claimed it under the Homestead Act.'

Lucha swished the pointer like a whip. 'Unfortunately, just as illegal as Sam Hatcher's deed,' she said. 'Because the point is that the land was never settled by treaty, never paid for—nothing!'

Billy Murphy rose again. 'Lucha, get hold of yourself. You've heard about whistling women and crowing hens. That's the last whistle out of you, woman. I'm taking you home.'

'You aren't taking me anywhere, Billy.'

'I paid two hundred and fifty dollars for my lot!' Riordan, the liveryman, shouted. 'That ought to buy me some rights in this mess!'

'It does!' Lucha said quickly. 'It buys you the right to sue Sam Hatcher for the return of your money. And—General Lopez, will you explain?' She spoke to him in Spanish. 'I'll interpret for the general, in case anyone doesn't know Spanish.'

Billy Murphy was silent as the general arose. An expression of kindly tolerance softened his eyes. He would speak a few words, then pause while Lucha put it into English, then continue.

'I wish to express friendship and understanding towards all of you. Those who are worried about the presence of the Mexican flag need not concern themselves. The land will be sold to you, exactly as it is, for ten cents an acre. Town lots will be sold for a hundred dollars. Take all the time you need to pay me.'

Sam Hatcher came finally, spurs clanking,

to the front of the room. The general gazed calmly at him through his round spectacles.

'I'll make you *all* a deal, too,' he said, glaring out over them. 'I'll reduce by half what you still owe me. But anybody who tries to deal with the general, here—that fool better start packing, because he's gonna be moving out. Say that in Mexican, Lawyer Murphy, so the general will savvy.'

Lucha started translating, but General Lopez y Durán shook his head. 'I understand,' he said. He lapsed into Spanish and, with Lucha maintaining an undercurrent in English, said: 'If any money had been paid by your country for the land, the largest portion of it would have come to me. As you know, I was governor of the Estado de Camargo at the time of the flood. My title to the land goes back to a certain corporal of the army of Cortez. Now, I don't wish a war with the United States, so I do not propose to ask for troops to retake this land. I suppose I will be paid for the land by your government after a new boundary commission investigates the matter.

'Those desiring to purchase title to the land they occupy may deal with Señora Murphy, who will confer with my *licenciados*.'

'*Simms, will you tell this greaser idiot what you found?*' Hatcher shouted, as the general turned to resume his seat.

John Simms, redfaced, sweating, removed

his cavalry hat and came sheepishly to the front. The little belly he had grown while living here would not be penned up inside his coat, although his narrow shoulders still fitted it.

'Yeah, well, I'm a surveyor as you all know,' he said. 'I rechecked the boundary lines that the commission did twenty years ago, and I found they were all in order. Yes, sir. Monuments and pins where required, and witnessed, and all duly recorded at the county seat in El Refugio.'

Whit spoke. 'I came across some of those monuments after you set them up, and they were all new. Even the bronze pins were shiny.'

'And there are no lines or corners on record at the hall of records, as my father learned and you very well know, Lieutenant Simms. Mr. Hatcher, how many sections do you claim?'

'I own five hundred thousand acres of the State of Texas,' Hatcher said. 'And I promise you, you'll never see the day when one acre of it is claimed by anybody else!'

'You will if you're still alive,' Jackson said.

The general store owner and mayor, Zachary Lord, stood at his place like a grossly oversized student. He was a thin, hard-looking man with full sandy mustaches. He was the mayor, for what it was worth, and dressed the part in a coat, double-breasted vest, and cityish trousers.

People craned to look at him.

'Tell the general this,' he said. 'Marcus St. Clair never lied to me. I suppose I ought to be afraid of losing a good customer, Sam. But you ain't a good customer. You buy wholesale in El Refugio. When I do sell you something, it's because you came up short.'

'What are you saying, fool?' Hatcher demanded.

'Lucha, will you tell the general I'll pay him twenty dollars a month on my town lot till it's cleared?'

'Thank you,' Lucha said. 'Anyone else?'

Whit watched husbands glance at wives, merchants confer with other merchants. Then the liveryman, Riordan, got up, rubbing his brow unhappily.

'I'll set tight,' he said. 'Don't appear I've got much to lose, unless the general plans to try to throw us all off our places.'

'That's not the point, Tom,' Lucha said. 'The advantage in securing a Mexican deed is that when the land is acquired by the United States—which it probably will be—then it may be claimed by someone else. When the United States bought land from Mexico by the Treaty of Hidalgo, existing land rights were honored. That's the advantage—*owning* it—which you don't as things stand.'

Hatcher raised his head and looked several of the townspeople in the eye. 'Anybody else?' he said. He waited, and no one accepted the challenge. 'Then *I'll* say something. All of you

105

have been crossing my land when you left the basin. There'll be a five-dollar toll after this. Some of you are behind in your interest payments. That money is due, and I'll be taking steps soon to collect or foreclose. And as to any lunatic trying to claim *one square foot* of LLCC land—you better make it six feet by two, because that's all he's going to need.'

Billy Murphy walked toward Lucha and aggressively offered his arm. 'All through, Miz Murphy? Can I escort you to your office?'

'I don't need an escort, thank you.'

Murphy stared at her a moment, then confronted Whit. 'You've got a problem,' he said. 'There's a man here from the Texas prison system. He came to take you back. It's between him and you.'

Jackson smiled at Clane, who stood in back near the door. 'That's the way it's always been,' he said, 'Right, Clane?'

'That's right. There was a right time for you, and there'll be a right time for me. But I've got a paper. You don't have.'

*   *   *

People began leaving. A few dared to speak to Lucha about acquiring Mexican title to their land or houses. But most of them kept their heads down and shuffled out.

General Lopez spoke to Lucha, in Spanish: 'Then if we're finished, I'll drive home. Your

106

friend will see you to your office?'

'Certainly. *Adiós*,' Whit said.

'Thank you,' Lucha said, shaking the general's hand.

Then there were only the two of them in the schoolhouse. She stuffed papers in her father's portfolio, her face troubled.

'They're afraid!' she said. 'They may just stay on dead center, and it will all blow over.'

'Give them a few days.'

'And what about that animal from Terlingua who came to arrest you?'

'He came here to kill me, not arrest me. He's going to wait for the chance I won't give him.'

CHAPTER TWENTY-THREE

Whit saw Lucha to the little adobe building under a chinaberry tree, where the street tilted down to the river. Then he rode back through the town to the livery stable. The town had the air of a cemetery after a funeral. Small groups of people on the walks talked and looked glum. People had spoken to him as they walked from the school, but awkwardly, as though he were someone not quite respectable, or merely, like an undertaker, uncomfortable to be with.

Jackson understood. Nothing came easily in

107

Los Lobos. Dollars were as hard to pick up as drops of quicksilver. Everything that was not raised here had to be freighted in, and money crops were hauled out to the fort sixty miles away, and the larger towns still more distant. The bank loaned money as though it were blood squeezed out of a vein.

Underlying the town's shaky economy was land. And now even that was jeopardized. People were afraid to abandon the high-handed security Sam Hatcher offered. Many probably wanted to buy title to their land from General Lopez—but that would be inviting retaliation from Hatcher. No wonder they regarded Whit Jackson as bad news!

Whit dismounted before Riordan's Livery Stable. He had things to buy for the ranch and no way to carry them. He walked into the barn, a big dim room smelling of hay, grain, and horses. Through a large door in the rear he could see horses in a corral. Inside the barn, Riordan was having a drink and talking heatedly with three other men. He was a big man with a close-cropped gray head set forward as though he were about to charge. A bottle rested on the back of a buggy. They all gazed in silence at Whit as he approached, seeming unable to decide what their attitude toward him should be. Riordan finally thrust the bottle at him and said,

'Man, you've got more gall than a quart of malaria medicine! Walking the streets as if you hadn't just busted out of prison!'

Whit laughed. 'What are you talking about, Tom? I'm in Mexico! Nobody's got any authority over me here.'

'I hope for your sake you can make that stick,' Riordan retorted.

Jackson drank a little whiskey and handed the bottle to a middle-aged man who had sad brown eyes in a yellow-brown face. He was Wendell Hill, and he ran cattle on some land near Jackson's.

Hill said, 'I don't think Billy Murphy's wife has the sense to come in out of the rain. I've been paying on my land for twelve years. Don't that give me some right to it?'

'If I sold you a horse that belonged to Tom Riordan, Wendell,' Whit said, 'would that give you title to the horse?'

'But Hatcher was here before any of us!'

'He wasn't here before the Mexicans, and a Mexican still owns this county!'

'Okay,' Riordan said. 'Okay, Whit! But do you remember what happened when *you* tried to take some land away from Sam Hatcher? I should think it would be pretty fresh in your mind.'

The men all watched Jackson.

'I remember,' he said. 'But I'm going back today and try it again. Things have changed since last time. Marcus and Lucha have given this basin a shake. There'll be Government surveyors down here again. And what's going

109

to happen when word gets out that the basin is wide open and going for ten cents an acre? Every down-and-outer in Texas will start heading this way.'

'Lucha ain't Marcus,' said a very tall man, a rancher named Roy Farmer. Farmer seldom had much to say, but perhaps whiskey and anxiety had loosened his tongue.

'She's working from her father's papers, though,' Whit said.

'You're making a lot of fuss just to get yourself out of a tight spot, Jackson,' Farmer muttered. 'What about the rest of us?'

Whit laughed wryly. 'Get it out of your head that I'm the only one involved in this, Roy,' he said. 'I think Hatcher's got you all scared foolish. He put this county together, for his own needs. He didn't want any big ranchers, and not too many small ones. He wanted people poor, and he didn't want any other ranchers competing for cheap labor and driving up prices.'

'That's true,' Wendell Hill admitted. 'If that spread of his were cut up into three ranches—'

'It won't be,' Farmer growled. 'Are any of you men going to buy Double L Double C from Lopez? I'd like to be there to watch the fun the day you claim it—out of rifle range, that is.'

'There's no telling what will happen around here, Roy. But just to be on the safe side, why don't you put some money down on your ranch with General Lopez?'

Farmer snorted and walked away. Others began making motions to leave as the conversation took this personal turn. But Riordan suddenly said: 'No offense, Whit, but I'd like to know something. The fact is, we'd only known you a couple of years before you had your run-in with the law . . .'

'Right,' Whit said. 'And you'd like to know whether I'm really as innocent as I claimed at the trial. Because I *was* having trouble with Hatcher, so maybe I stole a few horses to get back at him.'

'Ain't that what Kramer said at your trial? I wasn't in El Refugio for it, but that's what I've always heard. That you bribed him to leave those horses with you and take off and not come back.'

'That's the way I remember his story, too,' Whit said. 'But why would he take the money and leave the horses, and then come back here and tell about it? Why didn't he just tell me to go to hell?'

Hill's bloodhound eyes watched him intently. '*I* was at the trial, Jackson, and I didn't know whether to believe him or not. Kramer said he was afraid that if he didn't let you have the horses, you'd kill him. I knew there was bad blood, so it wasn't too hard to believe.'

'Would you believe it if you heard the story from Kramer himself? Because there's a good chance you will.'

'I heard Aguirre's got him in jail over there.'

'Okay, and I put him there—Ramón and I. And after he tells the rest of the story, I'm going to get Hatcher for conspiracy. If Billy Murphy won't arrest him, I'll do it myself.'

They looked at him dubiously. Sam Hatcher had thirty or forty men on his payroll, so how could anyone say he was going to arrest him?

'How are you going to do that, Whit?' Riordan asked.

Whit remembered something Lucha had said to him that day in Terlingua. It had been a kind of slogan to him ever since.

'I don't know, Tom,' he said thoughtfully, 'but I'm going to do my damndest.'

Whit took another small drink of whiskey and then brought up the matter of the wagon. Riordan hesitated but finally brought out a horse and hitched it to a flatbed.

'Good luck, you damn fool,' he said.

CHAPTER TWENTY-FOUR

Jackson tied his saddle horse behind the wagon and drove down to Zachary Lord's general store. Ramón's horse was at the hitch-rail, and the man was standing in the thin winter sunlight with his shirt collar buttoned, smoking a small Mexican cigar.

'*¿Ya mero?*' he asked.

'Pretty soon. Are you going out with me?'

'Sure. There's going to be a lot to do, *patrón*. Not much to do at my place until planting time.'

Whit asked him to drive the wagon around to the rear to load the merchandise he planned to buy. Simms could be counted on to have ruined a number of things. He walked into the store. It was a dim, cold room smelling of dust, cold ashes, and the many fragrances of provisions, those of smoked hams and bacons overriding all the others. Zachary Lord, the mayor and merchant, was waiting on two women, and Whit drifted about the big room looking for things he needed. In the rear, on a rolltop desk beside a dusty window opening on an alley, a telegraph key clicked and rattled like a set of runaway false teeth. He supposed the news of his escape had come over that instrument.

He found a wooden packing box and collected lamp chimneys, cotton and manila rope, some blacksmith's odds and ends, and a hide from which to cut harness.

The women left, with uneasy glances at him, and the natty little mayor hurried over to Whit. 'Finding what you want, Whit?'

'All but one thing—credit. And I want to tell you I'm a damned poor risk.'

Lord cocked his head to the telegraph instrument and raised one finger. 'My call letters,' he muttered. He went back to the desk and copied down a message. Then the key fell silent. He set the message aside and riffled through some papers. He selected one and came back.

'This was the one about you,' he said. 'We didn't have a telegraph line when you left, did we? We were promised a railroad, and I suppose this is the first installment. The message spoke of "armed and dangerous." I hope you aren't dangerous, but I see you're armed.'

'Do you blame me?'

'Can't say that I do. Well, your credit is good, Whit. As long as I've taken sides, I might as well go all the way.'

'I suppose you might, after bucking the big one today.'

'By the way,' the merchant said, 'you just missed Billy Murphy. He sent a message to the Ranger office in San Antonio notifying them that you were here, and requesting advice.'

'I could give him some,' Whit said drily.

'He was pretty sour about the land thing. In fact, he asked me to pass the word that his farm was for sale!'

Whit frowned. He was thinking of Lucha, not Murphy or the Rangers. Through the rear window, he saw Ramón bringing the wagon up to the back door.

'Is he planning on leaving?'

'He didn't say, but I suppose so. He's had

this wild hair lately about going treasure-hunting in the Yaqui country.'

'Damn fool,' Whit muttered. He began looking again for provisions. Would he try to take Lucha along? Would she go? He hoped she wasn't foolish enough to do so. Lord moved around with him. Evidently his thoughts were keeping pace with Whit's, for he said:

'I hope she don't go, because we're going to need her here—aside from the almighty danger she'd be in. I suppose I always did take this mayor thing too seriously. I've clucked around about buying water from the Mexicans' pond and all that, attracting settlers ... but nobody ever listened to me. People around here don't seem to have any ambition.'

'Yes, they do. At least they did when they came. But they're afraid to stand up to a big outfit, and they've got used to living under a low ceiling.'

He bought staples, wondering what kind of mess he would find at the ranch. Ramón helped him carry them out. It was mid-afternoon. They stopped at the feed store and bought a few sacks of grain, then left. It would be dark before they arrived. He was hungry to see it again, but knew it would be a mixed emotional experience. Simms would have let everything go to hell, but there would still be the old tree before the small adobe-walled Spanish fort he had converted to a ranch house, the crumbling walls, and the squat *torreón* with its rifle-slots commanding the ground within a half-mile.

Ramón rode with him on the wagon seat, the horses trailing behind. 'Has the man left?' he asked.

'He told me he was leaving, but Hatcher said he'd talked him out of it. I imagine he'll be there, waiting to be nudged.'

'What about others?'

'Wouldn't be surprised.'

Ramón did not ask what he would do if Hatcher had sent some men over to discourage him from settling in. Whit had no clear idea of how he would handle it; but his general plan did not include being bluffed. He had strong memories of Terlingua, recollections of being bullied and of men dying in his cell block; and the star he was following did not lead to jail, nor did he see himself skulking around making feeble bluffs for a few weeks and then drifting on.

Marcus had convinced him he had the law on his side. So if anyone got hurt, it would not be his fault.

They wound southward with the river, then turned east toward a low butte. His home place nestled against the base of the butte. A lavender-gray light settled over the butte and the hills, which looked like peaks pinched up out of wet clay. A cold breeze blew cool and steady, and the small, scattered mesquites

116

stood thin and rigid against it. The Murphys' farm was off to the west, near the river. He wondered whether Lucha would be going out there tonight.

That bastard, Billy!

From a half-mile off, he made out his ranch house, barely discernible in the last light, a flat building with a low *torreón* like a small silo at the left-hand corner. They were moving along one of his main pasture fences. The barbed wire was broken at points. He saw no horses. The graze was poor, partly from overgrazing, partly because of the dry summer.

The building slowly merged with the night. A lamp went on in a room. The *torreón*, a guard-tower in the old days, was at the left end of the structure; at its right were a couple of usable rooms. Then it crumbled down to ruins at the far right. A big cottonwood tree was sketched vaguely against the dark sky. Whit reined up.

'*¿Qué pasa?*' asked Ramón.

'I'll ride in from here. You stay put.'

He untied the buckskin, picked up his rifle, and swung aboard. Then he jogged down the road that ended at the well before the house. He stopped near the tree. A lamp was burning in the main room, hardly a parlor. The structure was one long low building cut up into rooms like cells. He had broken down one inside wall to make a larger room, and that was where the lamp was burning. He tried to picture what Simms might be up to and attempted to fix everything in the yard in his vision.

There was the round, low wall of the well, a wagon over at the right. At the left, the horse trap ended in a gate. He could hear horses in the dark, see a few indistinct shapes.

Then a shot came from a dark window.

His horse snorted and went lunging backward. He left the saddle. Lying on the ground, he tried to see which window the shot had come from. It was the kitchen, he thought, and the gun flame had licked from the sill. He eased back the carbine's hammer, and waited. The Henry held sixteen shells.

Another shot roared, and he fired at the flash. He could hear the bullet caroming about the plastered walls of the kitchen.

'Simms! You damned fool!' he shouted. 'Throw your gun outside. I'm not alone.'

Simms might be drunk. In that case, being fired at should help sober him a little. But another shot came, this time from one of the rifle-slots in the *torreón*, just above ground level. The upper floor of the tower had caved in long ago, and Whit had stored feed in the room. He levered up another shell, aimed at one of the slots, though he could scarcely see the sights to aim, and carefully squeezed off the shot. The Henry jarred him the length of his body; he heard the slug ricochet off the adobe bricks.

118

On the other hand, he speculated, Simms might have pulled out, and this was one of Hatcher's hands. But if so, why not two or three men there to welcome him?

'Patrón?' he heard Ramón call, and heard his spurred boots jingle on the road.

'Here! Stay low,' Whit called back.

Then there were three shots from the *torreón*, from the same rifle slit, none of them very near him. *One man*, he decided. He lay flat, then raised his head and fired another shot. He heard this one banging around inside the round corner room. He put another shot after it. He could hear Ramón moving, angling off to the right to get behind the house.

Then he heard a horse snort, hoofs clattering, and finally a horse running. There was a barranca behind the fort which cut into the butte; he thought the rider was taking the trail that led up it.

He had little conception of time, but it must have been a half-hour since the fight had started when he heard a shot fired at the rear. It was fired from outside, he thought, and there was no return fire.

'Ramón?' he called.

'Se fué,' Ramón called. 'He's gone.'

But Whit crawled on his belly to the well before he raised himself to study the house again. The lamp was glowing in the big room, but the wick had burned down some and the light was softer. He moved out quietly and ran,

119

bent double, to the fort. There he crouched, listening, before he rose and looked through the window into the lighted room. A man lay before an old bent-frame rocker by a round table where the lamp burned. It was John Simms, lying on his back. The front of his shirt was soaked with blood. His rifle lay near him.

CHAPTER TWENTY-FIVE

Simms was dead, his usually florid face the color of bacon fat, his eyes staring at the *vigas* of the ceiling. Ramón dug out some coins and laid a big Mexican penny over each eye. They had been through the house with a lantern, and Whit had collected five copper rifle cartridges of a large caliber. They looked bigger than his own Henry ammunition.

'One thing's for sure,' he said. 'He was dead long before we came. He's getting stiff. If that was his rifle, it's been fired, but not for hours. We didn't kill him, and I don't think he killed himself. Let's take him to the feed room.'

They carried the dead engineer to the *torreón*, laid him on a couple of bales of hay, and wrapped him in a tarp. Then they went back to the parlor, and Whit put the lamp in the room next to it, the kitchen, so that they would have some light from it, but without being clearly defined in case anyone tried to get a shot at them.

There was plenty of liquor around, both Mexican mescal and whiskey, and he poured each of them a shot in a china cup.

'He wasn't a bad one,' he said, 'aside from being crooked as a mesquite branch. At least he knew when to quit. Here's to him.'

Ramón stood near the window, gazing out. A frosty crescent moon had risen above the butte. In the cold light they could see a few horses in the trap, as well as their own saddle horses standing unsaddled near the gate.

'He didn't quit soon enough,' Ramón said. 'Or when he tried to, Hatcher wouldn't let him.'

They spelled each other that night, a couple of hours on, a couple off. Whit watched the sun come up, then he went outside. The dawn was clear and cold, the air sweet as cider. He remembered the things he had liked about the country his first winter here—the flawless morning skies, the smell of dry grass, mesquite, and horses; and the quiet.

A half-dozen horses in the long funnel-shaped horse trap had come up to the house to look for feed. All of them were bone racks; he cursed the dead Simms and the live Hatcher.

'Let's get some feed into those animals,' he said to Ramón, who had come out.

They carried hay and grain from the tower room, where Simms slept under a tarpaulin. They broke open three bales, scattered the flakes, and Whit poured grain into a trough. While Ramón got some breakfast started, he went behind the house and looked around. The gunman had ridden a large, unshod horse with a lug notch in its right forehoof. He saw where the animal had stood tied to a mesquite stump. But the hard ground told little about the nature of the man's boots. It would not surprise him if Sam Hatcher himself had been the gunman. If he had merely had Simms killed, it would mean still another witness to be dealt with.

They ate cornmeal mush and fried salt pork, and drank chicory coffee. Whit found a grain sack and into it dumped most of Simms's belongings. There was a cowhide valise, and he loaded it with Simms's personal gear—shaving things, silver hair brushes, a lot of personal truck he had probably carried around while he was in the Army.

Then they loaded everything, including John Simms, into the wagon. Ramón drove, with his horse tied behind, and Whit rode. He carried a fencing tool, plus wire and staples, to make a start on fence repairs. Now and then, on the way to Los Lobos, they would stop and repair a break in the fence. It was noon before they reached town. People stared at them as they passed, seeing the long bundle on the wagon bed. They stopped in a block of low, parapet-roofed buildings. Above one door was a sign:

and, in smaller letters: *Coffins. Undertaking.*

Several men came out of the Lone Star Saloon, next door, and watched as they let down the tailgate of the wagon. One of the men was eating a sandwich, others held glasses of beer. It was lunchtime. One man was in shirtsleeves and wore a long brown apron. It was Stu Perry, the furniture maker who had been at the meeting yesterday. He came forward, holding a half-eaten sandwich.

'Looking for me, Whit?' he asked, sounding curious. His skin was ruddy and smooth, and there was a faintly furtive quality in his grin.

'I've got a job for you, Stu,' Whit said.

He saw a man turn to call something into the Lone Star, and others came out and stood on the walk. Two more emerged from the barber shop beyond the saloon, and a couple of women stopped below it and watched. Perry finished the sandwich in a couple of gulps and asked, his mouth full:

'What's up, Whit? Is that furniture, or?—'

'It's not furniture, Stu. It's John Simms.'

'My God!'

Whit saw a stir of excitement, wonder, and pleasure go through the onlookers. They moved closer.

'What the hell happened, Whit?' Tom Riordan called.

123

Whit asked: 'Is Billy Murphy in town?' He and Ramón dragged the long, dark bundle to the tailgate. 'This is his department.'

Perry spoke to another man. 'Run down to St. Clair's office, will you? I think Billy's down there with his wife.' He wiped his hands on his apron. 'Here, I'll help—some of you men want to give us a hand with—with this? What happened?' he asked again.

'He was murdered.'

CHAPTER TWENTY-SIX

They carried the tarpaulin-wrapped corpse to the rear of the store and laid the bundle on the floor. It was covered with shavings which perfumed the air with pine and oak. There was a workbench, tools, saw-horses, and pots of glue, where Perry plied his trade of furniture-making and cabinetry. And there were two full-sized unpainted coffins and a child-sized one stacked against the rear wall.

Perry pulled on horsehide gloves, changing personality as he did so, becoming brisk and professional. Then he unwrapped the body, and men crowded close to look at it. Whit sat in front, in a rocking chair, and waited. He heard them swearing and exchanging observations on Simms's condition. By the time they began drifting to the front, where he

124

waited with Ramón, Billy Murphy and Lucha arrived. They came inside, Murphy looking displeased, Lucha perfectly blank.

'What is this, Whit?' Murphy demanded loudly. He looked at the Henry rifle standing against a chest of drawers near Jackson.

'This is a murder, Billy,' Whit said. 'We found him stone cold. Ramón will back me up.'

Lucha sat on a chest near Whit and looked at him, as the sheriff strode to the rear. 'Don't let him make you angry,' she whispered. 'Don't say anything you don't mean.'

Murphy came back, leading a ragged procession. 'Good God!' he said. 'He must have been shot point-blank. Is that the gun?' He nodded toward the Henry.

'No. That's mine. Simms's gun is with his things, in the wagon. It's a Winchester.'

Murphy leaned against the wall and looked at Whit, and at Perry, who had come forward. 'He must have been shot with a cannon,' said Murphy. He chewed his lip.

'Fifty-six Spencer would be my guess,' Whit said. 'Here are some empty cartridges I found near him.' He dug the casings from the pocket of his jacket. Murphy checked the markings on their base.

'I wonder if he might have shot himself,' he said. 'The muzzle blast scorched his shirt. He was in a bad state of mind after the meeting yesterday. And drinking, too.'

125

'If he shot himself,' Whit said, 'he lived long enough to fire at Ramón and me for twenty minutes. And those shells don't fit his gun by a mile.'

'Well, what happened?'

Whit told them about the encounter. 'I checked for hoof-marks this morning, and there were only the prints of one horse, a big one with a break in a fore-hoof. Ordinarily a man would leave his horse in front, at the rack or in the corral. So it was an ambush.'

'Huh!' Tom Riordan, the liveryman, scowled. 'Simms have any kinfolk?'

'I don't think that's the point right now,' Lucha commented. 'The point is, who killed him, and why? You're going out there, aren't you Billy?'

Murphy ruffled his curly hair. 'Hell. I s'pose I'll have to. Stu, you'd better get the doctor to dig the bullet out of him. It didn't come out the back. I looked.'

'I'll go,' a man said, and hurried away.

Then there was a stir at the doorway, spurs clinked, and onlookers moved out of the way as someone came into the opening. It was Sam Hatcher, big, unshaven, and rough-looking. He searched the faces of the group inside the shop, and then laughed.

'What is this—a wake?' he asked. 'I come to a saloon for a drink, and there's nobody there! Perry, you look like a church deacon. What's going on?'

Stu Perry said earnestly, 'Sam, John Simms—well, he's been killed!'

Hatcher shrugged. 'Well, that don't surprise me too much. How you doing, Jackson?'

Behind him stood Rip Clane and Hatcher's foreman, Dave Banta. Hatcher walked, spurs chiming, back through the room. Whit saw him gaze down on the dead man without emotion. He took a cigar from his shirt pocket and bit off the tip. Then he came back.

'Whew!' he said. 'Son of a bitch sure blew his gizzard out, didn't he?' He lit the cigar and dropped the match on the floor.

'Jackson says whoever did it fired at him and Ramón,' Murphy told him anxiously.

'Well, what do *you* say?' Hatcher challenged. 'Who's doing the investigating here? Hell,' he said, 'let's go next door and have a drink, where we ain't outnumbered by women.'

Lucha spoke as Murphy looked at her in anger. 'He has a witness, Mr. Hatcher. I hope you have, too. I'm sure my husband will want to know where you were last night. And the condition of your horse's hoofs—'

'What's the matter with my horse's hoofs?' asked Hatcher. 'He was walking easy the last time I sat on him.' But Whit saw a flicker of surprise in him. 'Come on,' he said. 'Ira, I want a drink. Let's go, men! We're going to drink to old John. God rest his soul.'

CHAPTER TWENTY-SEVEN

They had drunk to old John for a half-hour. The level in the bar bottles dropped steadily as the noise rose. As other townsmen came hurrying in, Hatcher had more bottles set out and tossed another gold piece on the bar.

'Come on, drink up, damn it!' he roared. 'What is this? Jackson, you gonna set there looking like a sick preacher?'

Whit had already noticed Rip Clane leaving with a bottle of whiskey. He had heard him ride off. He wondered whether he was planning on a private party of his own. He sat with Ramón, Zachary Lord, and Tom Riordan, and although they were drinking they were being careful. The effects of the liquor were already evident. People were telling John Simms stories now. He was assuming the nature of a folk hero.

'Them hairbrushes of his!' recalled Dave Banta, a tall, spare man with a ragged down-curving mustache. He wore leather pants, a Mexican shirt, and a leather jacket, and stood at the bar with the bearing of the segundo of the biggest ranch in a big county. 'They was silver-backed, and he wouldn't ride a mile without them! He'd stay over at the main place with us sometimes, and he'd always bring them damned hairbrushes! Spend more time brushing his hair in the morning than—'

'And could he put away the hard stuff!' said Stu Perry. 'When Doc Edwards opens him up, he's going to find he's already so preserved he wouldn't rot in a month!'

'He'd been in a hard-drinking trade—the Army,' said Banta. 'Them hairbrushes! And his *boots*! Hey, you go look at them right now—you'll see he'd buffed them up before he blew his guts out! Ain't it funny how a fella will do that? Straighten everything up, shine his boots, then shoot himself!'

'I suppose it'll be up to me to track down his kinfolk,' Sam Hatcher said. 'He had a daughter some-place. Nashville, was it, Dave?'

'Memphis. He used to get letters. Didn't she send a picture one time?'

'Hell, I don't know. Simms was the mysterious stranger, as far as I ever knew. I thought he'd make something out of that horse ranch of mine—pardon the expression, Jackson—but like a lot of other Army men he was mortally lazy. Let everything go to hell. Now I'll have to fix it up and put somebody else on it.'

Murphy came over to Whit's table and grinned. 'You gettin' all that, Whit? *His* horse ranch? Speak up.'

'You don't have to talk big to speak up, Billy.'

'I want to see them shells!' Hatcher shouted. 'Billy, you got them shells Jackson said he found? I want to see how old they are! Years, I'll wager.'

Outside, a horse loped up, and a moment later Rip Clane walked inside. He had been gone about twenty minutes. He went to where Hatcher stood at the bar. Whit rose as they began to mutter together, and poured himself a drink from Hatcher's bottle.

'Talked to Kramer, and he's in sad shape,' Clane was saying. 'That greaser sheriff Ageery wasn't there, and the place was locked up tight.'

'Did you check at his saddle shop?'

'Everything's closed for the siesta. I tried to get the bottle through the bars, but—'

Hatcher saw Whit. The older man turned to face the room and raised his voice.

'Hey, shut up a minute! Rip Clane went over to pour Hank a drink, and he says that little Mexican piss-ant of a sheriff's gone off and left him there to rot! He needs cheering up. Come on—we can be there in ten minutes.'

'Not so fast, Sam!' Mayor Lord raised both arms for attention. In his gray coat, loose wide collar and necktie he had a cityish look.

'That would be interfering in Sheriff Aguirre's business, Hatcher,' he said sternly. 'I wouldn't fool around in San Felipe.'

'Why not?' said Dave Banta, herding some men toward the door. 'Aguirre's just a Mexican saddle-maker with a tin badge.'

130

'And the authority to back it up, same as Billy Murphy used to have here. You go to tampering with his prisoners, and we might wind up with some Federals riding over. They've got jurisdiction here, too, you know—hell of a lot more than Billy.'

'I've got to see that day!' boomed Hatcher, draping an arm across Clane's and another man's shoulders and walking, laughing, toward the door.

'You're just a visitor, Hatcher,' said the mayor. 'Until you make a deal with General Lopez, like me and Tom done.'

Hatcher snorted. 'You too, eh, Tom? I'll stable my horse somewhere else after this. Come on—this ain't getting any rotgut into Hank, men.'

Whit, Ramón and the mayor watched the saloon empty. Then Whit got up. 'I'll ride along,' he said. 'You'd better stay here, Ramón, and keep an eye on those things of Simms's.'

'Don't get involved in anything, now,' the mayor warned Whit.

'Kramer's getting ripe. This might be important.'

*   *   *

At this season there was little water in the river, and the log-and-stone bridge upstream went largely unused. The road avoided the bridge, where the riverbed was deeper and narrower, and crossed through sandbars and mossy serpents of water a hundred yards below. Some twenty men, not all walking steadily or riding their horses soberly, crossed and swarmed up the road into San Felipe.

The pueblo looked deserted. All the shops were shut tight for the three-hour siesta. Venancio Aguirre's saddle shop on the plaza was still padlocked. The jail was a box of adobe bricks and broken stone on a back street, a tiny office hardly larger than a lean-to adjoining it. A ladder lay on the ground. The crowd made a riotous arrival, Hatcher rattling the locked door of the office, then kicking it; and then they milled around to the weed-grown side yard where the single window was. Whit stayed in the front rank.

The jail was intended primarily to house obstreperous drunks rather than criminals, but it was tightly made. The small window was a crosshatch of strap-iron bars with inch-and-a-half crevices riveted at the crossings. A man's fingers clutched the bars, and Hatcher yelled.

'Hank, you old horsethief, whattayuh say?'

Whit could hardly make Kramer out—the square-hewn Indian features, dark hair, and staring eyes. 'Listen, Sam—get me outta here!' Kramer said hoarsely. 'I'm sick.'

'Gonna take care of that,' said the rancher. 'I've brought you some of what you need. Put your mouth close to the bars and open wide!'

He uncorked the bottle he carried and thrust the neck through the bars. It gurgled and dribbled through, most of it spilling, and Kramer could be seen to open his mouth wide and try to close his lips on the neck of the bottle.

'Attaboy, Hank!' Banta yelled. 'Hang and rattle, man!'

Whit picked up a rock. He moved in close, and as everyone cheered Kramer on, he brought the rock down on the bottle, and stepped back.

The whiskey bottle shattered, Kramer cried out in pain, and Hatcher turned on Whit, his hand dripping blood. Whit backed off, his hand near the butt of his gun, knowing he had taken a big chance and that in the next few seconds something would be decided. Hatcher's face was pale and savage.

'You Godly son of a bitch!' he said bitterly. 'Throw down on me!'

On the edge of his vision, Whit saw men stumbling back, getting out of the line of fire. 'Señores!' someone said. Hatcher winced, revealing something important: he was afraid to draw his gun first. He was no fast-draw artist, especially with a cut hand, and if Jackson turned out to be faster—well, Banta and Clane might get Jackson, but Sam Hatcher would still be dead. He knew that.

'Draw, you horsethief!' Hatcher said again. He was saying to his men, *Get him!*

But they were all too close, and not ready—all in the line of fire, unsure of what this lunatic convict might be up to, and preferring to stay out of it.

'Señores,' the voice said again, 'I beg of you to behave yourselves! You are in Mexico, señores.'

'Who the hell—where—?' Hatcher stared around like a blinded bear wanting to charge. Whit looked up, remembering the ladder at the front of the jail. Sheriff Aguirre stood on the parapet roof with a shotgun trained on the crowd.

'I am asking you, señores,' he said, like a peasant general speaking to his rabble army, 'to depart. Return to your homes. This man is my prisoner. I have sent for the doctor. Do not meddle in my affairs and I will not meddle in yours.'

'He's right, Sam,' Stu Perry said. 'Look, Sheriff, we were just hoorawing the man—no harm intended.'

'Of course not,' Aguirre said, small and dignified but as determined as any man with a shotgun in his hands could be. 'The man will be taken care of. So you can depart, now.'

Men began backing away, stumbling over the rocky ground. Hatcher shook his fist at the Mexican.

'You take care of this man, Aguirre, or I'll be back here looking for you! You take care of him, or by God I'll take care of you!'

'*Por supuesto*,' said Aguirre.

The delegation to save Hank Kramer from the snakes wandered back to the plaza. Whit mounted, saluted the sheriff, and called up:

'Tomorrow morning I'll be back to talk to him, with a lawyer. Will that suit you?'

'As long as I am present.'

CHAPTER TWENTY-EIGHT

There was not a human being in sight in San Felipe, as if a plague had scoured the town of life. But Whit found the *zaguán* of the Hacienda Hotel and walked through it into the courtyard. The stable door was latched but not locked, and he went out back to check on his Mexican horse. It was still there. It was certainly not much, but Marcus St. Clair had bought it for him, and it had sentimental value. He would take it back when he went out to the ranch, and in the meantime he might as well lead it across the river and stable it overnight at Riordan's.

He was hungry, but the restaurant would not be open for another hour. He curried the big roughneck of a horse and found the battered saddle he had ridden home on. By the time he was through tending the animal it was after three. He walked down to the café and had an early supper. He was waiting on Hank

135

Kramer now. When Kramer was ready, he would be ready. But that would probably not be before morning and perhaps not then.

Leading the horse in a cold, windy dusk, he rode to the jail and pulled up outside Kramer's cell. Aguirre had a lamp burning in the office, and he could see the cowboy's shaggy head outlined against the grille as he stared out.

'I don't like doing this, Kramer,' he said. 'But I've got to get that prison sentence lifted, legally. You're the only man who can do it for me.'

Kramer spat through the bars and yelled a curse.

'When you tell people how it was—how much he paid you, the whole works about the other night, too—then we can talk about letting you out. But right now you're in trouble, and there won't be any booze until you talk.'

'Go to hell,' Kramer shouted.

'I'll see you in the morning, then. This is your last chance for a drink today. If you're ready to tell us, I'll rustle up a lawyer and a bottle of tequila before you can say Sam Hatcher.'

'He's dead.'

'Hatcher? Oh—the lawyer. Yes, but his daughter's filling in for him. She's a lawyer, too. Do you want to tell us about it? Get it all straightened out before supper, and then have a drink and something to eat?'

Kramer banged on the strap-iron grille with his palms and disappeared from sight. Whit cursed him and rode on.

Riordan was closing the big double doors against the coming night and the cold as he jogged up. There were lights in the houses of the town, and they looked warm and inviting. Riordan gazed out at Whit.

'My God, are you still alive?' he said. 'I keep waiting for a gunshot—'

'Will you put me up?' Whit asked. 'I've got a horse and a half, and if you've still got a cot in the office—'

'As a matter of fact, I've got a message for you from Lucha Murphy. I was just looking for you at the saloon. Come on in.'

Whit rode in, leading the other horse. As he dismounted, Riordan brought an envelope from his feed room, where, in an atmosphere of dusty grain sacks and horse liniment, he kept a desk stuffed with papers. The envelope bore Marcus St. Clair's letterhead, and was sealed with red wax, like a legal document. Riordan grinned.

'Looks like she don't trust me. Actually, I was down at her daddy's office on business, and she gave me this as I left.'

Whit didn't ask what the business was. He opened his clasp knife, slit the flap of the envelope, and took out a sheet of heavy paper and a key. In brown ink, Lucha had written:

Since you're staying in town, you might as well use the couch in the office tonight. And you'll be safer. Don't tell anyone you're using it. Billy and I are going out to the farm, but will be back by ten or eleven tomorrow. Here is the key. Love—

He refolded the letter thoughtfully and dropped the key in his pocket. Love . . . Damn you, Billy Murphy!

'That's quite some horse,' Riordan said, looking at the blue roan.

'A Christmas present from my lawyer. It doesn't need to be stalled, but I'd like the buckskin inside. I'm going to sleep at Marcus St. Clair's office tonight, but keep it to yourself.'

'I was going to offer you my office cot, but as long as you're fixed up— If you need your horse for any reason, the little door in the big door ain't locked.'

In the cold darkness he walked back through the town toward the river. A melancholy that was part fatigue settled on him, the reaction from too much emotion. I would like this to be over and done, he thought. I'm not a gunfighter; I'm a horse man. I want to be doing what I do best. What would it be like, he wondered, to live a civilized life with a woman? To have someone there besides a hired hand in the evenings? And some good and tender moments when

138

you just sat and looked at each other, dreaming.

Oh, damn you, Murphy! But if it hadn't been Billy, it would have been somebody else. Men wouldn't let a woman like Lucha stay single long.

Then he saw a light in St. Clair's street window and thought he heard Murphy's voice!

Did I read her letter wrong? But there was the cold iron claw of the key in his pocket, and as he drew closer he could see light above the green half-curtain drawn across the lower portion of the lawyer's window. He could hear Lucha's voice, too, low and intense. They were arguing.

He stood before the door and scratched his neck. Did Billy know she'd invited him to use the office? Should he barge in on a fight?

The door opened, and Murphy stood in the lamplight, coatless, his dark hair rumpled and his mouth surly. 'What are you waiting for?' he said. 'Saw you pass the window. Come on in.' He flapped some papers he held.

Lucha was sitting at her father's big cherrywood rolltop desk, wearing spectacles. He had never seen her wear them before, and she looked, with her hair pinned up and her lace collar secured with a gold clasp, like a schoolmarm—but a young and pretty one not much older than her biggest pupils. That small hint of vulnerability somehow endeared her to him. She took them off and smiled wearily.

'I thought we'd be gone by now,' she said. 'But we've been going over some business of Billy's—'

Murphy swatted his leg with the papers. 'Hatcher's getting too damn big for his britches! A whole raft of papers he wants served! Fifteen of them!'

'On who?' Whit asked. He turned a chair with his boot toe, and sat down.

'Everybody. Everybody that's delinquent in his payments to him, and who isn't? I'd be delinquent, too, but Lucha has some cash from her father.'

'So what's the problem?' asked Whit.

Murphy slammed the papers on the desk. 'The problem is I'm friends with these people! Serving a paper on a man is like hitting him in the mouth. *Fifteen!*'

'I told you, Billy, you don't have to,' Lucha said, laying down her eyeglasses. 'It's a county marshal's job, and there is one at El Refugio. Send them to him.'

'I don't need you to tell me, woman! That's the *law*. Fine. But how's Hatcher going to take it? I couldn't have been elected without him.'

There was an uncomfortable pause. Murphy stood at the window, glaring out into the darkness or looking at his own truculent reflection.

'I'm sorry about the other day, Billy,' Whit said. 'I shouldn't have lost my temper.'

'Me either. But sometimes—' He turned,

140

grinning crookedly, handsome and unpredictable. 'How'd *you* like to be married to a lawyer?' he asked.

'Don't know. Might be interesting.'

'Oh, it's interesting! Hey, listen!' Murphy said. He drove a fist into his palm. 'I've got a golden opportunity for you. How'd you like to buy a farm? Eighty-eight acres of good bottom-land near the river!'

Whit glanced at Lucha. 'Your place?'

Murphy went to the desk and pulled out a drawer. 'Where did Marcus keep his whiskey? Here it is.' He uncorked a bottle and took a drink, offered it to Whit, who accepted the bottle.

'*Permiso,*' Whit said to Lucha with a wink.

'I'll sell for three hundred dollars cash. But it's got to be gold. If I could sell it tonight, I'd do it. And be gone before tomorrow night.'

'Where?' asked Whit.

'The Yaqui River, in Sonora. Gimme that bottle, gunfighter.' He laughed; he seemed actually to have forgotten the harsh words and actions that had passed between them.

'And what about me?' Lucha asked. 'Where will *I* stay?'

'You're going with me.'

She crossed her arms. 'I am *not* going to Sonora. I am *not* leaving Los Lobos.'

'The hell you say. Damn these papers! He swept them from the desk to the floor and paced to the window again, like a prisoner in a

141

cell.

'Why don't you talk to Hatcher?' Lucha suggested. 'Maybe he'll buy the farm. He's the only one with that kind of money.'

'Don't talk like an idiot! I'll see to Roy Farmer in the morning. He adjoins us, so he'd be the logical one to buy it.'

'Farmer hasn't any money. He's one of the men you're going to serve papers on.'

The sheriff glared at her, then turned to Whit in frustration. 'Do you see what I mean about being married to a lawyer?'

'Oh, I'm sure he does,' Lucha said, rising, 'and I'm sure of something else. I'm not going to the farm tonight. It's too late and there's a lot to be done in the morning. I'm going to stay here, and right now I'm going to bed. Whit—'

'I don't give a damn what *you're* going to do,' Murphy said. 'I'm going out tonight. I'll stop at Farmer's on the way. I'll talk to a couple of other men tomorrow.'

'John Simms's funeral is tomorrow at noon,' Lucha said. 'You could talk to people afterward. I imagine most of them will be coming in.'

Murphy grabbed a heavy jacket from the leather couch. 'And I can just see myself selling farm land at a funeral! Think about that land, Jackson. You could raise your own grain—or, you know— Maybe the bank in San Felipe would loan you the cash—with all your

Mexican connections.'

He gave Whit a sardonic glance, walked out the door and slammed it. A moment later they heard his horse in back, scuffing off toward the river road . . .

'Well . . .!' Lucha sighed, picked up the office lamp with its green glass shade, and her glasses. She looked at him with the light warm on her cheek. Whit dug the key out of his pocket.

'I can bunk at Riordan's,' he said. As he pressed the key into her hand, he felt her palm and was surprised at the softness of it. The small touch, the warm contact was electric. And somehow the sight of her eyeglasses, too. He knew suddenly that she was also feeling something.

'I'm sorry about the couch,' she murmured. 'You could stay, but—but of course you couldn't.'

He closed his hand on her wrist, and she looked at him. 'No,' he agreed. 'People would say, "Whit Jackson's in love with the lawyer-lady. Why, she's already married! It's outrageous."'

His fingers probed and found her pulse. Her eyes seemed to grow paler. 'Normal?' she asked.

'How could it be, when everything else about you is so special? It's two hundred and ten.' He bent forward and kissed her lips. He could feel her breath on his lip and hear a little sigh. 'You were all I had to dream of!' he whispered.

She leaned against him, resting her head against his shoulder. He groped for the lamp, found it, and set it on the desk so that he could hold her.

'You had that girl,' she murmured.

'You and Marcus were all I've had since I came here. And you were married; and then Marcus died. Quite a month in Terlingua, that was. If somebody'd told me—God!—that as early as January I'd—'

Lucha turned her face up and kissed him.

He crushed her against him, his hands roaming her back. 'No—!' she whispered. He held her tightly and rocked her back and forth. Then he took her face between his hands and kissed her cheeks, her lips, her eyes. He drew her to the couch, protesting, and sat her down. She let her head fall back, as he kissed her throat and ran his hands over her shoulders and arms . . . She moaned and began pushing at him weakly.

'No, Whit—listen, dear, we—'

He took himself almost physically in charge and moved away, sat with his head in his hands for a moment, then rose.

'We've got to work something out,' he said. 'If he stays, Jackson's got to go. Does Billy love you?'

'I don't know! But you must go now. He might come back. We've got enough problems—'

He reached down, stroked her hair, and walked to the door.

CHAPTER TWENTY-NINE

Most of the little town was in darkness, with only a worn horseshoe of moon climbing the black sky. The bite of the air was invigorating; his face felt feverish. Murphy! Get out of my life! he thought, and groaned. The heel of his fist hit a pebbly wall at his side as he walked. Lucha was so strong in him that he felt she must hear his thoughts.

Murphy would get himself killed sooner or later, or vanish along some crazy treasure-trail. But how long could Whit wait? After prison he had had his fill of waiting for things; he was done with daydreaming.

He wanted her now.

A lamp was burning in Zack Lord's, and he stopped and peered inside. The lamp rested on a small safe beside his desk in the rear. He had not known the merchant left a night-light burning. He tried the doorknob on impulse, but the door was locked.

Shoulders hunched against the cold, he walked on toward Riordan's. A couple of doors before he reached it, he thought he saw the door open. Yes. A man came out, closed the door, and walked off up the street.

'Tom?' Whit called.

'Yo!' called the man. But it did not sound like the stableman. A moment later he was not there. He had vanished between two buildings. Whit drew his revolver and jogged up the walk. When he reached the door, he could see the space around it lit with yellow. He knew Riordan did not leave lamps burning—not in a stable—and tore the door open and let out a shout.

The bedding hay in one of the stalls was on fire.

He closed the door quickly to help close off drafts. The flames were blazing against the wooden slats and posts at either side of the stall. A horse in the stall next door was rearing and snorting. Jackson climbed the bars to cut it loose by unlocking the big harness snap that held it neck-tied to a crossbar. The horse went bucking down the aisle toward the rear.

He found a hayfork and started dragging the blazing hay into the aisle. Horses were snorting, whinnying, and stamping. He pulled out all the burning hay, then sank a bucket in one of the water barrels and started extinguishing the wooden bars that had already caught fire. They sizzled and steamed, and a sour smell filled the air. He poured water until there was not a spark left, nothing but steam. As a horse-raiser, he hated the sight of fire. He wouldn't hire a man who smoked;

he would have to chew while he worked for Jackson.

He lighted a lantern as the flames burned down and the barn began to go dark. With the Colt in his hand, he went out and looked down the alley between the barn and the building next door. No one had heard the uproar or his shout. He extinguished the lamp, set it down, and walked carefully to the rear. There was another alley in the back running right and left, and a maze of corrals. The horses moved nervously.

But the man who had set the fire was long gone.

Clane. Clane used to use the word, '*Yo!*'— and it had sounded like his voice.

He went back, locked the small door from the inside, and made himself comfortable on Riordan's cot, which smelled of horse liniment. Exhausted, he fell asleep promptly, with a gun under his pillow.

CHAPTER THIRTY

At the upper end of town, under a low hill, stood the small adobe church. Weeds bristled on its earthen roof. Behind it, on sloping ground, slept a tiny graveyard inside a flimsy picket fence. The church was of plain adobe, with blue sills and doorway, and the population of the graveyard was eighteen. At noon Whit walked up with Riordan, Zachary Lord, and Stu Perry. A circuit rider preached at Los Lobos once a month, but the time of John Simms's death had not coincided with his visit. So Perry, the undertaker, would read a service from a prayer book.

The grave was already dug, and Simms's flag-draped coffin rested on sawhorses outside the church. It would have been impossible for six men to carry it two abreast through the narrow door. Sam Hatcher, Dave Banta and some other LLCC cowboys stood near the coffin. Clane was among them, but not acting as a pallbearer. Lucha stood with some other women and a few children in the neighborhood of the grave, behind the church but in view.

'All right,' Perry said to Hatcher and the others, 'we might as well get started.'

Hatcher took off his hat and glared around. Was it possible, Whit wondered, that he was feeling guilty?

'If we're gonna do it,' Hatcher snarled, 'let's do it.'

The pallbearers carried the box around the corner of the church and up the hill to the cemetery. Whit and the others followed. They had discussed Riordan's fire that morning.

'I suppose I'll be next,' Zack Lord said. 'I'll sleep in the store for a few nights, and by God if anybody comes through that door he'll know he's in a fight!'

'You won't be alone,' Perry said. 'I told Lucha Murphy this morning I wanted to put some money down on my place, just in case. She said she's got some papers made up, with General Lopez's signature, to start things for anybody that wants to.'

'Where did you see her?' Whit asked. He wondered whether Billy had come back, for he was not here.

'At her daddy's office.'

'It's her office now,' Riordan said. 'At least I suppose he left it to her, not her and Billy.'

'Her,' Perry said. 'I asked her. A little money, too, I reckon. Well, wish me luck,' he muttered, walking ahead to join the group at the graveside.

In a loose ring they surrounded the raw gash in the earth and the trestled coffin. Stu Perry stood self-consciously in the black suit he kept for such occasions. A few women, who Whit guessed probably had not known Simms from Adam's off ox, dabbed at their eyes.

Perry laid the book open to a marked place and began reading. Whit heard a horse in the village below, a late arrival. Billy Murphy?

' " . . . *A little sleep, a little slumber, a little folding of the hands to sleep,*"' Perry intoned. ' "*Man dieth, and wasteth away; yea man giveth up the ghost, and where is he?*"'

The flag on Simms's coffin was far too small, and the wind was blowing it askew.

'"*All flesh shall perish together, and man shall turn again into dust*,"' the undertaker read in a nasal voice. '"*All his days are sorrows, and his travails grief*."'

A woman sobbed. Whit watched the Hatcher crowd. Clane was scowling, Hatcher looked stern, Banta crossed his arms and appeared perplexed.

The horse was still coming.

'"*There the wicked cease from troubling; and there the weary be at rest*."'

'Get it said!' Hatcher's voice growled impatiently, and several women gasped and looked at each other. Whit was amused. Hatcher leaned over and took the shovel from the pile of stony earth, impatient to be burying the dead man. Was he afraid Simms might knock on the side of the box, and whisper the name of his murderer? Hatcher looked gray faced and angry.

Perry read on, unperturbed, and Whit wondered whether he was deliberately prolonging the service. Heads were turning to look for the horseman; he was out of sight behind the church, and there was something eerie about the steady, unhurried clop of his horse's hoofs.

'"*What man is he that liveth, and shall not see death?*"' Perry read, looking out over the mourners. '"*His breath goeth forth, he returned to his earth; in that very day his thoughts perish*."'

Now Whit caught motion. The horseman appeared at the corner of the church, halted, and swung down. It was Sheriff Aguirre, from San Felipe. Come to pay his respects? As Stu Perry read on, Aguirre walked carefully up the slope to the graveyard, his big silver spurs chiming.

'"*In sure and certain hope of the resurrection unto eternal life—*"'

Perry closed the book and bowed his head. Hatcher's voice said, 'Pick it up! Get to it.'

His men started wrestling the long crate into the grave. There were no ropes to lower it with, and in the end the box was more or less dumped into the hole. Hatcher pitched a couple of shovelfuls of earth on top of it, handed the shovel to Clane, and said in rough piety: 'He was a damn fool, but a good man. Worse men are still walking the earth.'

Perry stared at him. 'It don't call for that kind of remark, Hatcher. But I agree with the sentiments.'

As Clane started shoveling in the earth, Lucha left the group of women and joined Whit. Sheriff Aguirre arrived, removed his hat, and crossed himself. He was murmuring, '... *Sanctificado sea Tu nombre ...*' and then in a low voice said:

'It is time.'

'Time, Sheriff?' Lucha asked.

'My prisoner wishes to make a statement.'

'Good!'

151

Some of the mourners commenced drifting toward the church. But Sam Hatcher shouted, 'Don't go away, folks! I've got a little sermon to make, too. I may not get a chance to talk to so many of you good people again.'

From his coat pocket he pulled a folded paper. Men and women halted in amazement and turned back, staring, but Clane kept shoveling. The pebbles clattered down on the coffin.

'In the beginning there was only me and Colonel Ed Drum,' Hatcher said, glowering about. 'That don't include barbarians. We curried the burrs out of this country and hung some Comanche hides on the fence to warn off the rest. They done for Colonel Ed, finally. Then you people began coming—from Texas, Arkansas—God knows where. You asked me for land. I'd bought this land from the United States Government, and I wasn't about to break it up like an Indian pot. I saw the time when I might need to put it back together.

'So I leased to you—'

'Ninety-nine-year leases!' called Mayor Zack Lord in an angry voice.

'Subject to your abiding by the conditions of the lease!' retorted Hatcher. 'Interest payments made regularly. The land to be improved. No attempt to be made to change the conditions of the lease. *No attempt to be made!* That's where some fools have stuck their necks out. Not to mention the condition some of you have let the land fall into. Tell them what the penalty is for violating any of the aforesaid provisions, Miz Murphy.'

'Cancellation,' said Lucha.

Hatcher raised his arm like a prophet. 'The lady lawyer says: *Cancellation!* And when people start reneging on their interest payments, and telling me they are buying the land from some greaser general—by God, friends, we are talking about *cancellation!*'

'You don't own the land, Mr. Hatcher,' said Lucha. 'So how can you subject someone else's land to certain conditions?'

Hatcher went a few strides toward her. 'The Texas Rangers will be here in a day or two to explain things to you, Miz Lawyer Lady,' he said. 'But all's you people need to know for now is that anyone who makes a deal with that Mexican breaks the deal with me. And he will be expelled from his land in the day that I hear of it. Does that sound churchy enough for the present occasion? In the day that I hear of it, I will come with some men and forcibly evict you from my land. Or my store. Or my saloon. And I will sell again to someone who understands the conditions better than some of you seem to.

'Clane, let one of Simms's town friends finish that.'

The Double L Double C men trudged from the graveyard. Dave Banta caught Whit's eye, shook his head, and shrugged. He's weakening! He won't back him to the limit! he thought.

Aguirre was murmuring in Spanish: 'And so if you will go with me now, I think he must have alcohol soon, or go into convulsions. He is very sick.'

'We'll stop by my office and I'll get some writing materials,' Lucha said.

CHAPTER THIRTY-ONE

Whit stopped at Riordan's to borrow a buggy. He left the horses there and drove toward the river end of town. Somber-looking men were trooping into the saloon to talk it all over. The Hatcher crowd had left town. He went into the saloon and bought a pint of whiskey.

Lucha was standing on the walk before her little office building under the leafless chinaberry tree, holding a large leather portfolio and an ink-case. Whit jumped down and handed her into the buggy, holding her hand after he did so. Then he drove toward the river crossing.

'I haven't seen a thing of Billy,' she said. 'But somebody's been in the office since I left. The safe has been opened.'

'Broken into?'

'No. I'd left it unlocked. I was getting out copies of leases and other business Daddy

154

wrote for people around here. There was a tin box with cash in it. Some of the money was gone—gold and bills. There was about eighteen hundred dollars that Daddy had told me about, and after his death I counted it. Five hundred dollars is gone.'

'A nice round sum to go treasure-hunting with,' Whit said.

Lucha looked straight ahead, holding to the grab-iron as they went through a rough patch of road. 'I *hope* it was Billy,' she said. 'I was already disillusioned, so I have nothing to lose there. But now—'

Now he won't come back, was the way he finished it.

They passed through the shallows of the river, took the road up into San Felipe, and Whit drove along the plaza and toward the jail. Sheriff Aguirre could be seen in the doorway, waiting. Whit heard muffled shouts. Then: 'Aguirre! You rotten lying chili-picker! You take that message to Jackson, Goddamn you! You ain't stirred out of here, have you?'

Whit threw down the buggy anchor and jumped to the ground. He took Lucha's writing gear and helped her down. They went into the jail. It was a small room with the cell door in one wall, the upper half of it a grille of strap-iron bars riveted together. Kramer came to the window and clutched the bars. The room smelled of vomit. Kramer yelled a profane greeting at Whit.

155

'I am sorry about the condition. He has a bucket, but he threw it at the door,' Aguirre said.

Whit confronted Kramer. Unshaven, the man had a fur of black stubble on his gaunt, high-boned face; his hair was tangled.

'Goddamn it,' he shouted, 'did you bring me anything to drink? *Aguirre, they're digging through the roof again!*' he screamed. He stared upward at the cracked plaster ceiling.

Whit found a terra-cotta mug on the sheriff's desk. There was a bucket and dipper, and he poured some water into the cup, then added a liberal dose of whiskey. Aguirre opened a small gate in the lower portion of the barred door. Whit called through it: 'Hank! Take this.'

Kramer reached for it, held it in both hands, and drank it all. Then he collapsed on the stool and rested his head against the wall. Lucha spoke.

'Hank, I'm Lucha Murphy. The sheriff says you're willing to make a statement about what happened before Whit Jackson was arrested. If you'll tell us, I'll copy it down and you can sign it. Will you do that?'

'Can't write,' muttered Kramer, already relaxing.

'Just your name?'

'My sign.'

'That's all right, we'll all witness it.'

'Write it down—what Jackson said at the

156

trial. Some more, Jackson.'

Whit poured him another drink and passed it through the gate. 'That's it, till we finish our work.'

'Then what?'

'Then in a couple of days you can go free. I'll lift the charges. All right, Sheriff?'

'*Claro.*'

Lucha seated herself before the door, the portfolio open on her lap and a traveler's inkwell fixed to it. She wrote: '*I, Henry Kramer, of Los Lobos, State of Camargo, Mexico, depose and state*— How did it start, Hank?'

Kramer sounded as though he were talking in his sleep. ' . . . Said—get rid of Jackson. Wasted too much time. Shorty said kill him, but—Hatcher said make an example of him, without stirring everybody up.'

'What were you to do, Hank?'

'What I done. Shorty spooked and took off. Only bad part.'

'How much did he pay you?'

'A hundred dollars. And a job. Long as I wanted it.'

'Did he ever threaten you?'

'Don't remember. He don't talk much. Sleeps on the roof. Keen as an animal. He's from Tennessee.'

'Then what he said was you were to join Mr. Jackson on the trail, and then take off. You were to come back and tell the sheriff you'd been threatened. You were supposed to say that Jackson wanted to sell the Hatcher horses to get even with him, and you'd divide the money. You were to leave then—go away. But you were afraid Whit Jackson would kill you at night even if you agreed, so you left after dark. Is that right?'

'Close enough,' Kramer said. 'Oh, Jesus. I feel better.'

'So do I,' said Whit. 'Hank, let's drink to this, and then when Mrs. Murphy is finished you can sign it.'

Kramer waved a contented hand.

*   *   *

They went back to Lucha's office.

Lucha opened a letter-press volume used for making copies of documents. She placed the confession on a blank page and over it laid a damp cloth. Then she arranged it in the letter-press, spun the wheel and clamped the volume solidly under pressure.

'There!' she said, with a sigh.

'Mrs. Murphy,' Whit said, 'you're a wonder. Your father would be proud of you. I'm proud of you, too.'

He started to kiss her, but she held him off, whispering, 'Wait! Someone is coming.'

'Lucha!' a man called, and there were other voices, and the sound of boots and spurs. Zack Lord appeared in the doorway. Lord was carrying a yellow sheet of paper. He was still dressed in dark funeral clothing. With him were Stu Perry, Tom Riordan, and big, lumbering Roy Farmer.

'Excuse us, Lucha, Whit—this may be pretty important. A telegram just came in from Ranger headquarters in San Anton'. It's in answer to the one Hatcher sent asking for a Ranger detachment to—well, arrest Whit and set things to rights.'

Whit looked at the men's faces, and his belly griped. They were all excited, all anxious, and the undertaker-furniture maker was working his hands together as though they ached.

'What do they say, Zack?' Lucha asked.

Lord's hands trembled slightly as he read the message the telegraph key had brought— the bombshell someone had prepared a hundred miles away, an hour ago, and launched by copper wire across the Big River, over the hills, across the brush thickets.

LOS LOBOS AREA NOT BELIEVED UNITED STATES TERRITORY. SUBJECT OF PRESENT INVESTIGATION. CONTACT MEXICAN AUTHORITIES REGARDING JACKSON. LETTER FOLLOWS, BARNES, CAPTAIN . . .

'So it's come down from the capitol!' Lucha said. 'Viva Jackson! Welcome to the Republic of Mexico, *amigos mios!*'

'But what's it do?' cried Farmer from the

159

walk. 'Are we all shut out? Will the Federales chase us off?'

'No! You heard what General Lopez said the other day. You'll have to pay him a very nominal—'

'What's that?' Farmer interrupted anxiously.

'Inexpensive—cheap. Ten cents an acre, on time, and you own the land. At the same time you can sue Los Lobos Land and Cattle Company for the money you've already paid, plus interest. Sam Hatcher doesn't own *any* land now, but he owns thousands of head of livestock and probably has plenty of cash on hand.'

'Will you write that down, Lucha, so we can study on it?'

'I'll have notices printed. In the meantime, I'm going to talk to Sheriff Aguirre about starting an action against Hatcher for conspiring to frame Whit. We'll have to bring in a Mexican lawyer from the outside. But you're all safe! Just go on about your business.'

'Will we have to take out Mexican citizenship?' asked Stu Perry. 'I don't even speak much Spanish.'

'I don't know. But you'd better buy your land before somebody else—Mexican or American—does. Why don't you all write your names on this sheet of paper—' She turned to the desk. 'It may be—I wouldn't be surprised—that the United States will sign a treaty with Mexico formally buying this land.

160

But in the meantime—'

Whit watched them line up to sign. 'There's just one thing,' he said. 'Hatcher claims all this land. Billy Murphy was about to serve papers on all of you when he took off.'

'What papers?' asked Farmer, startled.

'Demanding back payment of interest, for one thing,' Lucha said. 'He may be hoping to scare everybody out of trading with Lopez y Durán. So the big question,' she said, 'is, what are you going to do about it?'

Silence. Men crowding closer, looking at Lucha, at Whit, at each other. Looking fearfully down the barrel of the gun that had killed John Simms, Whit suspected. They looked at him hopefully. *Say something helpful, Jackson!* They were merely businessmen, farmers, ranchers, not gunfighters. Why should they have to risk their lives to make a bare living in a hip pocket of Texas—no, Mexico!— in a lost town like this?

'I've got some reason to go out and talk to Hatcher,' he said finally. 'I'd like to arrest him for conspiracy to send me to jail—for setting me up for Kramer to kill the first night I was back. I've got strong feelings about Sam Hatcher. But we're in Mexico, you see? So how can I—an American?'

'In the first place, you can't go out there alone, for *any* reason,' said Lucha.

'But if he don't know about the telegram—' began Stu Perry.

'He knows,' said Roy Farmer mournfully. 'Dave Banta was in the saloon when you brought that telegram in. He gulped down his whiskey and left like his tail was on fire. Excuse me, ma'am. It's only an hour's ride out there. Oh, Hatcher knows by now, all right.'

Whit took his revolver from the holster and squinted at it. He rocked the hammer back and forth and watched the cylinder turn. Then he glanced solemnly at Riordan, laughing inside.

'If I had a few men to go with me—partway, that is—till he spots us . . .'

'Lynch law? A shootout?' Lucha asked, exasperated. 'Absolutely not! This doesn't have to be done today, or tomorrow.'

'I've got a feeling that the more time he has, the more things are going to happen. Happen to me, maybe. So face it now—lock him up. Say, I know what I'll do!'

They waited, fascinated but fearful.

He holstered the gun and chuckled. 'I don't know much about Mexican law, but I'll bet Aguirre would deputize me if I asked him to. Just pin a badge on me, and let me do the rest. What do you think, Lucha?'

'I think you're insane!'

'If I rode out there,' Whit said, thinking about it, 'I'd want some of you men to go with me. Then it would go one of two ways. One, they'd take off when they saw us. They're ordinary cowpokes, and not being paid to die.

Two, some of them would stay. Clane will stay because that's why he came—to get square with me.'

Perry adjusted his spectacles. 'But what if most of them *do* stay, Whit?'

'Well, if we left pretty soon, we'd be arriving about sundown—the light would be in their eyes. They might fire from long range to scare us off.'

'Then what?' asked Lord.

'Give them a couple of days to think it over. I figure they'd soon be hauling out of there the first time Hatcher turned his back. Thirty dollars a month doesn't buy much blood. So all you've got to decide,' he finished, 'is whether there's enough at stake for you to risk your lives backing me up—right now.'

'I'll go,' Lord said promptly. 'And, Tom, you certainly must be in it after last night.'

Riordan scratched his neck. 'He might have wiped me out. You know I'm in it—up to my eyeballs. It'll be dark in less than two hours, and it's an hour's ride out there, so—'

'I'll tell you what,' Whit said. 'I'll get Aguirre to deputize me. Pass the word to anybody else that might want to be included. I'll be back in a half-hour.'

Then, in front of everyone, he kissed Lucha's cheek and walked from the office.

CHAPTER THIRTY-TWO

With a solid silver star, Sheriff Aguirre made a Mexican deputy out of him. Then he got out a bottle of tequila with which he had been dosing Hank Kramer and poured a couple of fingers in two glasses.

'To your good health, *diputado*,' he said.

'Hey! I'll drink to that, too!' Kramer yelled through the barred window in the cell door.

The sheriff shrugged and poured a drink for Kramer, passing it through the gate below the window. The sheriff and Whit touched glasses, and Kramer laughed wildly, drank, and pounded on the door.

'Hey, listen!' he shouted. 'Gimme another shot and I'll drink to your good luck! You're gonna need it, feller!'

'You said he sleeps on the roof,' Whit recalled. 'Is that true?'

'Damn right it's true! And don't you know he's got an arsenal up there?'

'How's that?'

'Old Colonel Ed had a crate of guns he brought along when he left the Army. Henrys—not regulation—damn sight better. Load 'em on Sunday and fire all week. Gimme another shot, Ageery. We ain't going to see this man alive again. He needs all our good wishes.'

Aguirre gave him another drink. Then the

164

sheriff shook hands with Whit, who finished his drink and left.

Riding back to Riordan's, he thought about the lay of the land out at that fortress of Hatcher's.

The main house was at the crest of a low sweep of land. There was a collection of Mexican adobes, like kennels, that he called bunkhouses. The corrals were off to the right. There were no trees because things like trees and bushes were a weakness. There was a windmill behind the house and a cement water tank on the crest of the ridge.

Before the livery stable, a group of eight or ten men, all carrying rifles, waited on horseback or beside their mounts. The shadows of their horses sprawled across the road. A couple of the men wore bandoliers of ammunition. Riordan gave Whit a box of shells, which he poured into the fence-staple pouch behind his cantle.

'If the warden could see you now,' said Tom Riordan.

Whit looked over the group. 'How many of us are there?'

'Ten, with you. Aguirre didn't want to come?'

'I didn't ask him to. It's our fight, not his. Kramer says he's got a whole crate of Henry rifles, and that they'll probably use the roof as a parapet.'

They set out, the horses acting up with the

excitement.

The road ran north, then northeast toward the higher ground. The distant hills were already lavender in the late afternoon. The dust of the horses drifted with them in a cloud. Hatcher would know they were coming, and be waiting.

'How do you figure this?' Riordan asked. 'He could put men out as skirmishers, couldn't he? Pick us off . . .'

'The land's too flat for an ambush, but he could set a few snipers.'

After a half-hour Whit saw dust ahead. The on-coming riders were a quarter-mile off.

'We'd better make a skirmish line,' he said, pulling up. 'If they look like they mean business, we'll dismount.'

They spread out over a line a couple of hundred feet long, and waited. The dark point of horsemen widened, became a ragged file of riders, fifteen of them, perhaps twenty. Whit waved his rifle and swung down.

One of the horsemen jogged ahead, his right arm raised. With the pink light on his face, he was finally recognizable. It was the foreman, Dave Banta.

'I want to talk!' he shouted.

'Leave your men and come ahead!'

Walking a few yards in advance, Whit waited. Banta, the big, gaunt segundo, jogged his horse to within twenty feet of Whit and pulled up.

'Jackson!' he said, 'Is that you?'

'Excuse the star,' Whit replied. 'I'm a deputy now. What's going on?'

'We're leaving. The old man took a couple of shots at us before we could get clear. Can I come closer?'

'I can hear you.'

'He went wild when I brought him that telegraph message. Had us all get our rifles. Then he went up on the roof with a crate of rifles. I told the boys to make up their own minds—stay or quit. Clane decided to stay. We saddled and got the hell out, but one of them took a few potshots at us from the roof when they realized we were leaving.'

'*¡Ven acá!*' Whit said.

Banta rode up. He carried a revolver and a carbine in a boot but was wearing gloves—hardly the equipment of a man who planned to make a fast draw.

'What do you think he's planning?' Whit asked.

Banta shook his head. 'He'll never quit, I know that. You won't take him alive. He was up there on that roof, but God knows where he is now. Maybe on the hill.'

'Maybe. I'll tell you, Banta—prison must've made me suspicious. Light down and leave your guns here. Then call your men up, one by one, and have them do the same. Then ride on.'

'I hear you, Jackson.'

Banta dismounted, dropped his weapons on

167

the ground, and rode back to his men. One by one they rode up, laid down their weapons and waited. Only a few had rifles or carbines. There were eighteen of them, eighteen unarmed men now standing restlessly by their horses.

'Go ahead,' Whit said. 'Ride on to town. I'll bring the guns in when we go back. Whenever that is.'

'That's fine,' the foreman said. 'Don't forget—he didn't take this country away from the Comanches by bein' dumb. I don't know what you're getting into. I'd tell you if I did. I just worked here, Jackson. But no more.'

CHAPTER THIRTY-THREE

The ranch house and outbuildings ascended from the earth. In the dusk, the main building was like a pile of mud blocks, the corrals still just pencil scrawlings at the right; the corrals looked like animal pens, and, behind it all, on the slight rise of land, stood a concrete water tower and a windmill. Whit knew the house would have a parapet roof like any other in this country, but did not know whether Hatcher, back in the Indian days, had cut rifle-slots in the parapets.

He called to the men to spread out. There were a few cattle here and there, horses becoming visible in the corrals. The sun was dropping behind a cordillera of rough hills in the west, and a bank of clouds behind the water tank flamed with orange and pink.

They jogged on.

At last all the buildings had definition. The water tower resembled a blockhouse. Whit could hear creaking noises from the wooden skeleton of the windmill. He thought of the graveyard where John Simms slept, nothing moving but dry weeds that the wind stirred. He stopped and raised his arm, and the other riders halted.

'Hatcher!' he shouted. 'I want to talk to you.'

He saw a flash and yelled, *'Down!'*

As he landed on his feet, a bullet struck the earth ten or twelve feet from him, spattering him with grit. He plunged forward onto his face and lay absolutely flat. The roar of the gun came and with it more flashes, more bullets striking around him, a wild fusillade from a single rifle loop. He lay with his arm before his face, while the gunman emptied a whole loading tube at him, sixteen bullets almost the size of his thumb. Before it was over, he knew he was in a very slight depression in the earth, since the bullets were landing some distance ahead of him, or behind.

'Jesus God!' he heard Zack Lord gasp, at his left.

The shooting ceased. Whit raised his head. A cloud of black smoke drifted south from the roof of the ranch house. He started to bring his rifle to his shoulder, but without warning another rifle winked, and another eruption of gunfire raked the ground near him, the bullets screaming and whining away.

He waited until the shooting ceased, counting the shots this time: sixteen, a full loading tube and a cartridge in the chamber. He searched for movement on the roof, but saw only the cloud of smoke drifting away.

Lord called nervously, 'How the hell can we ever take him? He can fire all night with an arsenal like that!'

'I'll work around behind the house. It's all we can do.'

'But they'll!—'

'It's only one man so far. I don't know what Clane is up to. I'll work around to the right, behind the corrals. There's a few wallows over there.'

'But!—'

The firing resumed, flaming, roaring, echoing, smoking—a madman's rage howling from the roof. 'Pass the word,' Whit called. 'He may show himself when I take off. Start firing as soon as I run—'

He picked out his next spot, a hog wallow with a little drying mud in it, glinting with orange light. When the rifle went silent, he scrambled up and ran for it. He heard Lord and the others begin to fire, the slugs whining off the adobe parapet. The gunman took one shot at Whit, and waited.

Whit pretended to rise and flopped down again. Hatcher, if he was the sniper, hurled another roaring fusillade at him. The instant the rifle went empty, the men with Whit began firing, and Whit ran. He made it behind a water trough beside a corral. He did not think he had been seen, but when the firing resumed, the wooden trough exploded into broken wood and a flood of water. Soaked, he scrambled behind a wagon. As he heard the men firing again, he sprinted on to the side of the house.

Ahead of him was the dark hulk of the water tank, the creaking derrick of the windmill, and the ridge. It did not look high enough for him to get in a shot at the roof. He looked at the windmill. From there, or the roof of the tower, he could pour down a fire that would roast Hatcher alive.

But where was Clane?

He crouched behind an adobe shed and measured the distance. Hatcher might be watching for him now; probably was. But the windmill would afford some shelter. The ladder was at the rear, a little platform thirty feet above, under the revolving wooden vanes of the fan.

It would soon be dark, and then God knew what would happen. Hatcher might descend through a crawl-hole, or by a ladder, and move among them or take off.

He could hear the others firing randomly from the other side of the house, stuttering hopeful shots at the rifle-slots. He crawled to the base of the windmill, then straightened and groped for the ladder. As he found the rungs, he heard a *thump*, then a man's voice above him: 'Damn—'

And a shot came down from the platform.

He dropped, realizing the sniper on the tower had been hit by a sail of the turning wheel. The bullet plowed the ground between his feet. He shouted, full of rage and fear, and began firing overhead. He heard the bullets shredding the platform. Another shot roared down, and he aimed at the flash and fired.

He heard a groan. Then a shape rose and launched itself like an owl out over the water tank. There was a splintering crash, a splash. He waited, his heart thudding. No more sounds came. Only one man had been up there, he decided. He started up the ladder.

Soon he could see the roof of the long ranch house. He searched the front wall, saw several rifles lying before the crenels through which the rancher had been firing, and some small wooden cases, probably of rifle shells. But no sign of the rancher.

He crawled out on the platform. A shot roared up and splintered a wooden vane behind his head. Another shot flashed and another. He sweated as he aimed into the slot from which the man was firing. With the barrel of the Henry resting on the floor of the platform, he squeezed and felt the hard kick of the gun.

One shot, a foot-long flash. Then a man fell back and lay outstretched on the roof, his body visible from the waist up. Fearful of some Indian-fighting ruse, Whit worked the lever and put another shot into the man, then another. Then he slowly stood up.

'Jackson! What the hell's going on?' someone bawled beyond the house.

'Come on. It's over,' Whit shouted back. 'Come around to the back.'

He sat crosslegged on the platform, waiting until his friends appeared. He remained there until they lighted lamps in the house and searched it. Riordan came out. It was dark now, and he carried a lantern.

'It's empty,' he called. 'Guess that's it.'

*   *   *

That was it. Whit stood up. He gazed steadily southwest, imagining he could see a winking light near town. Perhaps it was a Mexican rancher's hut, an oil lamp burning in a window. The thought of a lamp burning in a window lifted him. Tired to the very marrow, he started down the ladder.

We hope you have enjoyed this Large Print book. Other Chivers Press or G.K. Hall & Co. Large Print books are available at your library or directly from the publishers.

For more information about current and forthcoming titles, please call or write, without obligation, to:

Chivers Press Limited
Windsor Bridge Road
Bath BA2 3AX
England
Tel. (01225) 335336

OR

G.K. Hall & Co.
P.O. Box 159
Thorndike, Maine 04986
USA
Tel. (800) 223-2336

All our Large Print titles are designed for easy reading, and all our books are made to last.